JULIET WAS A SURPRISE

ALSO BY BILL GASTON

NOVELS
Bella Combe Journal
Tall Lives
The Cameraman
The Good Body
Sointula
The Order of Good Cheer
The World

SHORT STORIES
Deep Cove Stories
North of Jesus' Beans
Sex Is Red
Mount Appetite
Gargoyles

POETRY
Inviting Blindness

DRAMA
Yardsale

NON-FICTION
Midnight Hockey

BILL GASTON

JULIET WAS A SURPRISE

STORIES

HAMISH HAMILTON
an imprint of Penguin Canada Books Inc., a Penguin Random House Company

Published by the Penguin Group
Penguin Canada Books Inc., 90 Eglinton Avenue East, Suite 700, Toronto, Ontario, Canada M4P 2Y3

Penguin Group (USA) LLC, 375 Hudson Street, New York, New York 10014, U.S.A.
Penguin Books Ltd, 80 Strand, London WC2R 0RL, England
Penguin Ireland, 25 St Stephen's Green, Dublin 2, Ireland (a division of Penguin Books Ltd)
Penguin Group (Australia), 707 Collins Street, Melbourne, Victoria 3008, Australia
(a division of Pearson Australia Group Pty Ltd)
Penguin Books India Pvt Ltd, 11 Community Centre, Panchsheel Park, New Delhi – 110 017, India
Penguin Group (NZ), 67 Apollo Drive, Rosedale, Auckland 0632, New Zealand
(a division of Pearson New Zealand Ltd)
Penguin Books (South Africa) (Pty) Ltd, 24 Sturdee Avenue, Rosebank, Johannesburg 2196, South Africa

Penguin Books Ltd, Registered Offices: 80 Strand, London WC2R 0RL, England

First published 2014

2 3 4 5 6 7 8 9 10 (WEB)

Copyright © Bill Gaston, 2014

Author representation: Westwood Creative Artists
94 Harbord Street, Toronto, Ontario M5S 1G6

*Publisher's note: This book is a work of fiction. Names, characters, places and incidents
either are the product of the author's imagination or are used fictitiously, and any resemblance
to actual persons living or dead, events, or locales is entirely coincidental.*

Manufactured in Canada

LIBRARY AND ARCHIVES CANADA CATALOGUING IN PUBLICATION

Gaston, Bill, 1953-, author
Juliet was a surprise / Bill Gaston.
Short stories.

ISBN 978-0-14-319241-1 (pbk.)

I. Title.

PS8563.A76J84 2014   C813'.54   C2014-901271-3

eBook ISBN 978-0-14-319203-9

Visit the Penguin Canada website at **www.penguin.ca**

Special and corporate bulk purchase rates available; please see
www.penguin.ca/corporatesales or call 1-800-810-3104, ext. 2477.

To Lise, and love

CONTENTS

House
Clowns

He woke up to the challenge of a mountain sun blaring through thin white curtains. Without lifting his head from the pillow he took stock of the bedroom, feeling beyond it the empty cottage and a hollow presence that felt a bit too eager. It could go either way. He decided he'd better stand up, get right out there and see what came.

After morning ablutions, he searched the cupboards for coffee but found none. This was fine. Coffee was a mistake, especially now; even two cups hid a nasty tipping point. He was here to try hard. He had made these arrangements and driven all this way not just to find the old clarity but to keep it. He'd told no one. Strings of that sort felt like confusion.

Inside the backyard shed, beside some fishing rods, he hefted a wooden shovel, thick and designed for healthy work. He smelled a cool, grass-clipping mustiness, a waft of childhood. The question, Did I make a huge mistake choosing an urban life? came with a ripple of panic, which he quelled by stepping back outside. Bouncing the shovel, he scanned the lawn for a worm spot, some wild place that wasn't grass, shrubbery or flowers. There was nothing diggable all the way down to a wall of cattails and the lake. An inner voice asked almost sarcastically why he was breathing quickly, especially with all this stillness around him and a view he'd paid for and driven four hours to see. He brought his gaze up. Okay, there was Pinanten Lake, liquid black glass mirroring a dark mountain on the far shore. The lake was speckled with boats, people fishing. Trolling silently, eerily, the boats all had little electric motors. He'd read in the McGregors' leaflet that gas motors were banned.

The leaflet had also bragged of the lake's "world class trout." His sarcastic voice had relished telling him that the flip side to all this promised fishing glory was that there would be nothing else to do here. But he'd fish. He could do it. He could stab a hook into a worm and not be thrown off course by its writhing. He could reel in a trout. And fry one. Butter, flour, salt. He'd famously taken Casey fishing that time and got nothing, so if he caught a trout, he could call his son and tell him. It would be the perfect reason to call, all the way to Belgium. At the phone he'd joke lightly, a trout shining in the sink. "Casey. Remember how we went to Sooke and didn't catch anything? I've felt like a failure for years, so—" The call would continue perfect, lively with Casey's questions. None of which would ask if his mother was there with him, or was he taking his meds this time, or was this in fact a vacation.

The shovel wasn't tall, so he'd have to stoop. Last week, in a gesture to his coming great health, he'd thrown away his velcro lumbar brace. Without support, his back felt precipitous, a cliff of possible pain on every side. He pictured the movements of shovelling.

He recalled all the roadside bait signs. He would hunt worms in his car.

But the signs had proved fraudulent. At each gas station, Bubba's, the outfit that supplied the worms, was behind on deliveries. A clerk joked, "Maybe Bubba got into the beer," and "Bubba's probably lying in his hammock." And as it always goes with these things, when he tried the Bubba-into-the-beer quip himself on the next baitless clerk, the young muscleman threw his head back and squinted, hostile, possibly a relative of Bubba. He saw now that his journey had dangerous choreography.

He drove all the way into Kamloops, finally locating a prize tub of worms—in a 7-Eleven, no less—and learned from reading the tub that Bubba's Bait Inc. was a corporation with a website for an address. He wasn't sure what any of this might mean. He smiled at the notion that these might be multinational worms. But fishing now felt less pure, and less destined. At his car, in the rising heat of parking lot blacktop, he peeled open the tub's plastic lid to find in peat moss maybe eight thick, alarmingly flaccid worms, barely alive, the grey green of turned bologna. He pressed the lid back, seeing he could be nudged off the journey by worms. The flip side was that they didn't look capable of agony if he stuck a hook in.

HE MANAGED TO KINDLE some fishing spirit on the return drive. His clarity was deepening, and he noted with a nod the hawk eyeing him from a fence post as he glided past some dry fields. Then he saw, pulling into the carport, the cottage's front door ajar. This wasn't too disturbing, but as he got out of the car there were voices coming from inside. This wasn't necessarily horrible either; a rural place, maybe neighbours dropped by and such. What was bad was the voices stopping at the sound of his car door closing. Worse, they stayed stopped, and after a time he could hear whispers.

He stood beside his car, not moving, worm tub against his leg. He could turn now, get in his car and fly. But that was probably ridiculous. And he'd heard a woman's voice in there. Not that that changed anything, not these days. But this was all wild thinking. There was a clear reason for people to be in there. They wouldn't be the owners, since there was no car. Unless, a taxi. Their leaflet said they lived here winters and travelled summers. Maybe something had happened to their trip. But wouldn't they have phoned? They—

"Hello!" A young man popped out smiling, his hand already in a wave.

"Yes. Hi." His own hand came up automatically. The young man was twenty-five, thirty, and unshaven. Tanned, with startling blue eyes. Actually, he was extremely handsome. His T-shirt was filthy, his hiking shoes looked beaten up or even found. It was too hot for those jeans. His blond hair looked unwashed. But his good looks were male-model calibre. Who dressed like that with a face like that? His manner, the way he spoke, showed that he knew he was handsome.

"Fishin'?" The fellow glanced at the worms and lifted his eyebrows rhetorically.

"Bubba's," he answered, feeling stupid as he turned the tub to show him the lid. The leaflet said the McGregors had raised kids here, kids who had "loved the place," so maybe this was a child's ill-timed return. Now a young woman appeared too. Without looking at her, the man raised his arm to let her in, and she stuck her shoulder into his armpit. She seemed nervous and fixed her gaze on her boyfriend's cheek.

"Are you the owner?" asked the young man.

"I'm the renter," he answered, too keen to claim even that bit of ownership when of course he should have said nothing, seeing how the young man's question revealed so much. And now, at this answer, the woman turned his way with a beautiful, ripe-peach smile.

The young man said, "Hmm." It was too long a pause. "This is strange," he said at last. "So are we. The renters."

She continued to smile sweetly at him. That light in her eyes he knew he would take to bed with him tonight to dwell on, parsing it for what might be its defiance, or its dangerous lie, or—this was possible now, given his deepening journey— its beautiful welcome.

THEY WENT INTO the kitchen to "sort this thing out." Before sitting down, the man swung round to offer his hand. Introductions followed. The young man was Adam, his girlfriend Eden. She was not Adam's equal in looks. But her body was sinuous, and he had always had a weakness for white halter tops. Her spirit was eager and well tuned. He bet she got what she wanted. When the unlikelihood of their names dawned on him he froze, and Adam said, grinning, "I know."

"We get lots of jokes," said Eden. "But I mean, I could have been Eve?"

"You did have a long history of snakes," Adam said, pretending to glower.

"Oh, stop," Eden said, smiling down at her tea fixings.

This including him in such intimacy alarmed him even as it seduced him. It could be signalling the best, or the worst.

He left a polite amount of time, then gently slapped the kitchen tabletop. "So. Okay."

Adam looked up and agreed. "Yes."

Eden made to move behind him, ostensibly to get something. When he quickly scraped his chair back from the table to keep her in view, he hoped it looked like he was just trying to position himself to include her.

"Okay." This time he slapped his knee. "So you rented, starting today. For how long?" He had a series of questions ready, ones that wouldn't directly accuse them.

"A week," Adam said.

"So it's a double booking, then," he said, nodding. "It looks like they ... the, ah, what's their name—" He hoped his act of forgetfulness looked convincing.

"McGregor," said Adam. His knowing the name would have been a relief were it not for him pointing his chin at the stack of mail on the counter beside the phone. Why would he gesture to it unless it was his source of the name? And why had he gone through their mail?

"Did they charge you the same price? Five hundred?" He was especially happy with this question, though as he said it, he felt transparent. He saw them trade a glance.

"Um, I'm pretty sure we actually paid more, come to think of it. Didn't we, honey?"

Eden, brow knit, nodded. "I think it was more like seven, wasn't it?"

They got the price almost right—it was seven fifty—but they didn't look like the kind of people who spent that much money then forgot the exact amount. They had no car. Maybe no luggage.

"Sounds like you got a deal," said Adam, the humour in his tone maybe also a challenge.

He wanted to ask about the no car. He tried for the right words.

"Okay. So if we do decide who shouldn't be here, if we flip a coin or something, if it comes down to that—well, you seem to lack transportation?" He tried to look sympathetic.

"We hitch-hike. Or we just hike. We like it. See the country. Meet the people."

"Where are you coming from?"

"Calgary."

"I could drive you out to the highway if you lose."

"Hey—I'm not saying we're going." Now Adam wagged a finger at him, and the wagging grew to belligerent pointing. "We're not flipping a coin. We're here. And how do we know *you're* not some kind of—"

"Idea!" Eden stepped in, smiling brightly. "The McGregors. It's their mistake. When we tell them what happened, they'll make it up to us. A refund. They have to! And look at the size of this place. Two storeys, two giant bedrooms, giant lawn, lake. We won't even see each other if we don't want to. Half-price vacation. And hey, maybe even we all fall in love and have a time." She put a hand to her heart, peered ceilingward and batted her eyes. "Maybe in ten years we'll be writing letters to each other."

He didn't know where to look. Eden said all this in the easiest, funniest way, such a skilful overture of friendship that any response but acceptance would seem crippled, almost evil. Was there much danger, really? If the choreography was violent, wouldn't they have done it by now?

"Well, today it's too late for anyone to be leaving anyway," he said. He shrugged in a friendly way and lifted his eyebrows. "We can try calling them. The McGregors. See what happened. I think in their note they said they were travelling in Europe. I think France and Italy. I don't know how we'd ... maybe a neighbour?" He was babbling now. For one stupid moment he'd almost said he had a son in Europe, a son who could somehow help. He needed sleep.

"We know what happened," said Adam. "They double booked. Why bug them?"

"Maybe some neighbour would have a number to call."

Adam turned his teacup with fingertips in fast circles, the cup obviously hot. Eden gazed around the kitchen. He had not touched his own tea, nor had he thanked Eden when she put it in front of him.

"We can be your house clowns." Eden put her hands to her head like antlers and swayed back and forth, big-eyed and unsmiling. Her eyes were playful but ironic and—he didn't know why he thought of this word—literate. But still possibly dangerous. There weren't two bedrooms, there were three. None were giant. Anybody, especially any woman, knows exactly how many bedrooms they are renting. Vacationing renters don't hitch-hike. They just don't.

HE DIDN'T THINK SLEEP was in the cards, and he was right. He lay staring at the ceiling, blinking rapidly if he blinked at all. They didn't want him phoning the McGregors. They had no food, no car to go get some. It felt portentous for someone as handsome as Adam to dress like that. Even if—even if they were just a couple of hippies looking for vacant houses to crash in, as a kind of lifestyle, well, what kind of wimp was he? Why let himself be bullied like this?

In the deeps of the night his thoughts curled faster, possibilities he knew were less and less reasonable even as he thought them. Adam was the son he'd never had, a son who would find him wise and worth listening to. Eden would invite him to their bed and Adam would leave, nodding. Eden's nipples petalled out with Celtic-knot tattoos, and Adam's lower back bore a prison-ink swastika that, when examined under a microscope, proved to be the Upanishads in Sanskrit. They were roving cannibals waiting for a certain phase of moon, one he could discover only by reading the codes on the soles of their feet. Eden had used "house clowns" in the Shakespearian sense, and he, as king of this rental house, would receive flawless ironic instruction, emerging after a week humbled but clear-seeing and cured. Again and again he was surprised, tortured and killed in all manner of fresh ways. But most creative was how he was manipulated psychically. All these thoughts, for instance, issued from them. Even this one. These weren't his thoughts at all. These two were *clowning* with him already.

HE WOKE UP FULLY ALERT. It didn't feel like he'd slept much. An hour, maybe two, judging from the grit when he blinked. The smell of bacon wafted from below. He hadn't brought bacon. For now, it was their only message to him; he could hear no chat. He pulled on yesterday's clothes. He would shower and shave after he assessed things.

Out in the hall he stopped and checked his wallet. His cards were all there, and sixty-five dollars. Something was wrong. He thought hard. Yes—he'd returned yesterday with only forty-five. This should have been a relief, or even funny, except it hinted at the kind of subtlety these two might keep employing. Except, he might have had sixty-five. Had he bought the worms with cash or card? He pictured himself in that 7-Eleven. He could see the hotdogs rolling on their greasy rollers; he could see the two kids in line with their neon-coloured slushies. But he couldn't see what left his hand.

In bare feet, he walked lightly so they didn't know he was in the kitchen until Eden turned with her frying pan of eggs.

"Jesus!" She put her free hand to her throat. "You got me."

The hall bathroom flushed and Adam emerged, wiping his hands on his shorts. He was showered and shaven, and his clothes were clean. His T-shirt had a Prince of Whales logo with a leaping killer whale beneath.

It was not lost on him that Calgary lacked whales.

"Yay," said Adam, not smiling but eyeing the food hungrily. "Breakfast."

"Good-looking bacon," he said, just to see what they'd say. It did look good. Thick.

"Saw a sign a few miles back," said Adam. "Found a bike

in the shed and went lookin'. The sign said 'double-smoked.'
Still don't know what that means. Didn't see no smoke-shack
nor hog-butcherin' types lollin' about." He chuckled at his own
jokes while turning to get forks from the drawer. "But I got
those eggs too. Organic."

He went for his wallet. "Well, I think I owe you … twenty."
He watched them both closely.

"No, no. Get us later. And there's no way it's twenty."

"Hey"—Eden pretended to chide Adam—"it might be.
We haven't seen him eat yet. These skinny ones are the worst."

He offered his own polite chuckle as they chatted about
how skinny Japanese always won hotdog-eating contests, and
wasn't it strange that such contests were on the sports channel.
He helped set the table. He served himself at the stove. He
ate some bacon, eggs and toast after watching them eat first
and waiting a minute. Same with the tea they were drinking.
Though he desperately wanted coffee now. There was general
conversation about how they'd all slept. Adam had like a log,
Eden never did well in a new bed the first night, and he of course
had slept well, thank you. Eden's plans for the day involved
nothing more than lying in the sun, reading and "a giant cold
beer at four precisely." Adam was going to take the day as it
came, but might try fishing, and could he maybe mooch a few
of those worms? Then it was agreed that maybe he and Adam
would take the canoe out together and try for a big one. After
breakfast Eden and Adam did the dishes, hunkered down like
people trying to repay a debt.

Not saying where he was going, he slipped out and climbed
into his car. Once on the road, he was aware that he could

simply keep going. The clothes and whatever else left behind wouldn't add up to much. Or he could go straight to the police, though he didn't know what he'd say to them. And anyway, if these two did mean him harm it was beyond a police matter, it was personal, it was a choreography rising up from the deep forces that clarified all things.

He pulled into the Pinanten General Store. At one point he found he was smiling as he shopped, and this made him smile wider and shake his head. He bought coffee and fruit and something for dinner—a package of ground bison, tomato sauce, linguini, a lettuce head—and also a bag of marshmallows, he didn't quite know why, other than the orange-blue-yellow squares on the package seemed perfect, like he'd just discovered himself in a new land and this was its national flag.

When he returned, Eden was there in halter top and bikini bottoms, humming to herself as she bustled from cupboard to drawer, hunting something. Her breasts were truly quite fine.

"You came back," she said wryly, not having even glanced at him. She did a little grin now and looked him full in the face. "We're not so scary."

The sunlight coming in behind her worked like a halo, the gorgeous rainbow traces perhaps due to some imperfections in the glass. It was so overdone he could have laughed, were he not on guard.

"Coffee," he said, lifting his plastic bag to the counter. "And milk. And cherries. I found some at—"

"Coffee! Oh! Oh! Oh!" She ripped the can from the bag and rolled it against her forehead as one does a cold can of beer.

She panted with full tongue. She really was quite the comic. She checked to see that it was fair trade.

"It's in there," he told her, pointing to the lower cupboard with the coffeemaker after she began slamming through them one by one. He told her, yes, he'd like a cup himself, and he preferred it strong.

WHEN THEY WERE BOTH down at the dock, he went through their stuff. Both had mid-sized packs holding enough to take on a short vacation, but also an amount that could conceivably be all they owned. In hers, a well-thumbed Tom Robbins. A little hash pipe. Or crack pipe? No, he knew what a hash pipe looked like and it was a hash pipe. Why had his mind gone to "crack pipe"? Did something in him want it to be a crack pipe? Also, a little book of phone numbers. Would you take that on a week's trip? Maybe. And toilet paper. Why take that to a furnished house? Well, it might be a hitch-hiking woman's reasonable gear.

Now his knuckle bumped something cold. A pistol. So here it was. He threw his head back and let himself breathe deeply, extravagantly. Then he hefted it. It felt somewhat light. He moved to the window with a view of the yard. He could find no safety switch. He depressed a little button and out slid a magazine, shockingly full. He counted seven. Looking more closely, he saw instead of bullets the rather more impotent folded-up ends of what had to be blanks. A starter's pistol. For robberies? For two savvy travellers to scare away bad people?

Whatever the reason, it was a compact portrait of characters at home in the bad life. Here they were in his.

He went through Adam's small bag and it held only clothes, half of which were hers. So Adam was chivalrous. But why—a chill teased him—was there no ID? No wallets, money, cards. No one travelled without ID. Were they seasoned travellers taken to hiding it under mattresses? But why hide it in a rental cottage in Pinanten Lake? Why hide it from him?

The timing perfect, here came Adam striding across the patio. Checking that he left things the same, he made it to the upstairs bathroom before Adam's steps sounded in the kitchen. He locked the door, started the shower. He'd get in under the spray and think. But he'd be vulnerable, he could picture the door breaking open, he'd slip in the wet tub in an attack. So he sat on the toilet, pants on, and watched the door. He heard what sounded like the fridge slamming, then Adam's feet back outside on the deck. He stood and breathed and tried to gather reason to him. Clearly they weren't who they said they were. Clearly they had plans for him. What these plans were he had no idea. He was still open to the possibility that their intentions were good—were benevolent, in fact. They could be messengers, guides to what on this trip he was trying to relocate, they might be nothing less than a wonderful opportunity. Yet you could be tricked in precisely this way, by anticipating the best. God knows it had happened before. So he must assume the worst but be ready for anything. Stay alert, but open.

He did take his shower, feeling silly. It would be nothing so crude as smashing down a door and … and what? Stabbing him à la *Psycho*? He dried off, softly whistling, and dressed in his bathing suit and T-shirt. Flip-flops and UBC ball cap. He wondered if they knew he used to be a professor. He wondered if they'd done research on him.

He strode down the lawn, arms swinging, flip-flops flapping, midday sun instantly at work on his neck. Walking the damp path through the cattails to the dock, he heard their murmurs before he burst into view. Kneeling on her towel and topless, Eden squeaked and covered up with an arm. Adam, sitting on the overturned red canoe, snickered.

"Oops. Sorry," he said. He'd stopped with one foot on the dock.

"No worries. You scared me." Eden appeared to trade a look with Adam. "You ever been to France, sailor?"

It took him a moment to realize she was serious. He told her he had.

"No big deal then." She dropped her arm. Adam smiled at him benignly.

Wondering what this might mean on the deeper level, he knew at the same time that the protocol was to be casual, cosmopolitan. Crudely turning away was as uncool as staring. You didn't not look at them if they fell into your field of vision. He stood centre-dock with them in the periphery and he successfully kept them there. He could see only that they were very white.

"Fishing?" he asked Adam. "Or is it too hot?" He saw Adam trade looks with Eden again. "They don't seem to be feeding, though." He scanned the water, putting a hand to his ball cap brim as a silly extra shield to the sun. But he almost knew what he was talking about. Where today there were none, last night the many concentric circles out there on the surface had to have been fish sucking down bugs.

"Let's do it," said Adam, slapping the fibreglass of the canoe. He offered to go up and get the worms from the fridge and the rods and tackle box from the shed.

"Have you seen any paddles?" he called to Adam's trotting back, and Eden informed him they were under the canoe.

"Let's flip it," she said. "You flip and I'll catch," she added, positioning herself to face him but three feet away, across the red hull, no aversion of his eyes possible. He did as best he could to keep his eyes on hers; he wasn't going to lose this particular trial, whatever it was. As he flipped and she caught, her smile was knowing.

"If you can look down," she said, "you'll also see two life jackets."

"Yes," he said, and smiled as well, though it felt wooden.

"Could you please try to get him to wear one? He can hardly swim."

"All right."

"He'll deny it but he's a dog-paddler. He can barely get across a pool. A *width*."

"I'll try."

"You should put some of this on. You look hot." Eden flipped him a pink tube. "And could you put some on my back?"

He caught the tube. He watched her eyes as he undid the cap and squirted a dollop into his palm. Rubbing a dab onto his cheeks, he said, "No. I won't." He was pleased with himself, not only his restraint but his ability to see the buildup and interrupt the momentum at what was very likely an important juncture.

"Oh." She did a fine job of looking taken aback and slightly hurt. "All right."

They slid the canoe in, he not looking at her. He stowed the paddles. After donning one life jacket he threw the other in front, thus laying claim to the back, where a canoe was steered.

Adam came smiling through the cattails, carrying the fishing gear and a bag that held, he said, an apple for each of them. Eden made a plaintive joke about no beer, then declared that she also wanted to come on their little fishing trip. Adam asked if she was sure. He made his own little joke about pirate ships and females and bad luck.

"There's three seats." She pointed to the canoe. "It's ordained. And it's not like you're going to catch anything anyway."

"I was sort of hoping we would," Adam said. He looked genuinely hopeful, boyish.

As he watched Adam and Eden play their parts, he considered her use of the word "ordained," and the bag of apples, which was so biblical as to be funny. He wondered if the apples were planned, or spontaneous slapstick on Adam's part. And now the supposed change of plan, of Eden coming along. It occurred to him that no one, not a soul, except the McGregors—but who could say they weren't a part of this?— knew where he was. He hadn't told his wife, an omission that had felt vital at the time. As for his work, he was over two years into his extended leave, and most ties there had stretched and broken.

"Excuse me," he said. "Can you wait one minute? I have to go up and …"

Adam said of course, he had to get the rods ready anyway. Eden asked if he wouldn't mind bringing down a thermos of water or, she said in singsong, "something stronger." Stepping through the cattails he heard her ask Adam to put some lotion on her back.

He dug the number from the depths of his wallet. An odd European number with more than one area code, he'd dialled it perhaps three times in the half-dozen years since Casey had gone there. Theirs was a profound and troubling relationship, one where not calling always felt as richly significant as calling. He suspected Casey felt the same. They'd never been able to talk about meaningful things; their conversations resembled a small red canoe moving superficially across the lake of what mattered. Casey had been adopted. He was one of the first proofs he had received that nothing happens by accident. Seeming chaos was always choreography, but more complex, and more tightly woven. Your role was yours to find, and the barriers to finding it were towering—career, medication, psychiatry, the visible world, logic itself. But the truth was luminous. It was as exciting as magic.

And he was excited on the walk up to the house. The sun cooking his neck. The fabric of his shirt teasing his skin. The smell of the grass as it respired, sending his nose the choreography of water and chlorophyll. The bronze doorknob—he could feel tarnish though it wasn't raised, and though soundless he heard the inner springs and gears of the mechanism as he turned it. Clarity was getting more consistent, and closer.

As he'd hoped, Casey's voicemail came on. He found his son's voice unsettling; he'd never been comfortable with its higher register. Casey asked, in both English and French, that callers leave the date, time and purpose of their call. He sounded the crisp bureaucrat.

The voice caught him and he hesitated too long. He had to hurry through his message.

"Casey, it's your father. It's Dad. I'll be quick. I'm going ... I'm going fishing, trout fishing. I might be in some kind of trouble, I don't know. So if you don't hear from me again by tomorrow, I'm at Pinanten Lake, B.C., renting a house from the McGregors. Mom doesn't know any of this. Okay." He wondered what more he might say, until a beep sounded.

He found a thermos, held his finger under the tap as the water got cold and ran over his message in his mind, wondering what his son might make of it. He hadn't wanted to sound disturbing—or even worse, crazy—but he could think of no better way of telling the *truth*, so to speak. He'd only been accurate. Still, if Casey decided he was already in trouble, how long would it take for an address to be found and authorities contacted?

It occurred to him that it might have not only *sounded* like a cry for help but *been* a cry for help. Did some hidden, frightened shadow-self want police to show up tomorrow and ... what?

Well, if the police did come, he could always just show them that everything was fine. He could introduce them to his young friends. At that point he could check everyone's eyes, the police too, see if they pretended not to know each other, hopefully discover how far-reaching the scenario was this time.

He found himself gripping the door frame and staring into the hall closet, blinking, as if searching for something he needed for fishing. He truly needed sleep. The coffee hadn't helped, hadn't been good for him. He was deadly tired, yet on the opposite side of calm. He cocked his head to a crow yelling from the ridge of trees that separated the McGregors' yard from the neighbours', but he didn't know what it meant. He was getting frustrated with being unable to tell even a warning from a welcome. Generally you just knew, but when they sounded or looked identical, your only chance was to open up and see under the surface of things. Which had been the whole point in coming here.

Recalling from another time a trick for staying aware, he rummaged through kitchen drawers and cupboards. Peppercorns were good, but he found none, and in the end he settled on wooden matchsticks. He dumped a couple dozen from the box and snapped them in half. With duct tape he painstakingly taped all the jagged bits to his bare ankles and feet, tops and bottoms, binding them tightly.

Two perched crows watched him try to take normal steps as he navigated the lawn. The flip side to the matchsticks and duct tape was that he'd had to don shoes and socks to hide things. They were brown leather shoes and white socks and didn't go with his bathing suit or, he guessed, with paddling a canoe. He didn't mind being ugly but feared his outfit might give away that he was on to them and would not be distracted, no matter what lure or drama they used.

Halfway down the lawn he had an idea. He turned painfully and doubled back. In the fridge he found some mustard, the brownish European kind, and applied an earnest layer to his nose. He checked himself in the hall mirror and with a finger fashioned a pointed little flip of mustard at the nose tip. He would tell them it was a new and superior sunscreen from Germany. If they saw past this shield and asked about his wearing dress shoes in a canoe, he would tell them that the last time he'd been fishing his son hooked him in the foot, right between the toes. Anyone who'd suffered that would never fish again without shoes, he'd say.

He caught sight of himself in the mirror, and he smiled at the man with ball cap and sunglasses and ochre nose with its elfishly curled tip. Of course, if they were on his side—he still held out hope that they were—they'd understand these precautions. They could all laugh together after they revealed themselves. But he mustn't be deluded by this hope. That was what usually got him in trouble.

HE STROKED STRONGLY and alertly from the rear while Adam dipped a seemingly calmer paddle up front. In the middle, Eden kneeled in a regal posture, having joked about being an Egyptian queen. Her arms hung straight down from her shoulders.

He'd forgotten to bring water or beer but they'd forgiven him and Adam had sprinted up for three beers after Eden comically batted her lashes. Her top was back on. When Adam returned with three cans (and where had *they* come from?) he tried to commandeer the rear seat, saying he'd been a camp counsellor and could scull a canoe into a dock sideways, and quipped that men with yellow noses couldn't be trusted to steer. Neither of them mentioned his feet. But there was no way he was going to let both Adam and Eden sit behind him, let alone steer. He refused and told them that he was also expert, and once they'd cast off and paddled a small distance, he saw what it took to steer. Though he jolted them a few times he thought he did a fairly convincing job, but after the failed negotiations there on the dock, Adam and Eden pretended to be angry and neither spoke to him.

The water, the naked fact of floating on it and moving through it, was thrilling. Anyone's small shift of balance was instantly felt by the other two, a communication so intimate it wasn't unlike sharing one long body. When they approached the middle of the lake, he didn't like it when a fish jumped right beside them. It was a ridiculously large trout and such a blatant lure to "come fishing" that it felt heavily portentous and dark, especially as it happened in the deepest, most isolated part of the lake. Adam pretended to be excited by it. The plan had been to paddle to the span of reeds on the other side, because that was where most boats appeared to gather, but after the trout jumped, Adam wanted to fish right there and then. Eden had the rods lying to either side of her, and Adam asked her to pass him one.

But he ignored Adam and kept paddling, even when they questioned him. When he ignored them long enough, they stopped talking. So he was succeeding. They were learning who exactly they had taken on. He began to feel immensely proud, even to the point of taking deep, ecstatic breaths, which he noticed in time and recalled from the past and stopped. But not soon enough.

"Know what?" Eden said softly. "I think I'd like to go back."

He was careful not to change his paddle stroke. Adam didn't speak.

"I'm maybe feeling a little seasick, you know?" she added.

"Want us to turn around?" asked Adam, gently.

"I dunno. What do you think, honey?" She did a good job sounding vulnerable.

"Captain?" said Adam, rather too loud. "What say we head back. We can do this thing another time, maybe."

"No," he said. "I really want to go in … there." He lifted his paddle to point in the direction they were headed, a dark gap in the bank of reeds. He'd been watching it for some time. Yesterday he'd seen two canoes emerge from it. It was a stream or inlet.

"That's the channel I heard about," said Adam. He cupped a hand over his eyes, gazing like a sailor. "It goes to a second lake. Little Pinanten."

He wasn't sure if he liked that Adam knew about it, but he kept paddling. It wasn't far. He could see that the channel was no more than eight or ten feet wide. Now Eden was acting angry with Adam, who in turn acted excited about their new adventure, marvelling at how narrow the channel was, and how tropical looking, and then blurting, "African Queen!" Which might have been a mistake on his part, joining her earlier comment about Egypt and revealing the choreography in too broad a hint.

And only now, watching Eden kneeling no more than two feet in front of him, did he consider what he'd been taking in all along. Her hands resting on her thighs, her spine straight— this posture would be called "pert," except for the strategic, languid rolling of her shoulders in rhythm to their paddling. It was adept and perfect in its subtlety. Of course she knew he watched her. Her communication couldn't be more direct. Her bare skin, luscious tan. From her bum crack, peaking above her bikini bottoms, a tattooed blue hand waved at him. He could smell her, a confusing mix of scents. Appropriately, comically, a tackle box full of lures lay not an inch from her bum. They would know, probably to the month and day, how long he'd been without sex.

He saw how easily she could overwhelm him if he paid her any more attention at all. He raised his gaze. He wriggled his ankles to locate the many pains of the matchsticks.

He was almost certain now that they weren't on his side. And he sensed that whatever happened, good or bad, it would happen in Little Pinanten Lake.

About fifty yards from the mouth of the channel he began a careful, curving aim toward it. He had gotten good at steering. Everything was coming together smoothly. Even the several boats in the area, soundlessly propelled by their tiny electric motors, had been elegantly dispersing.

"It really might be fun," said Adam, pausing in his paddling to regard the approaching mouth, "to see where this goes."

Eden offered a sarcastic "Mmhmm."

Their acting was so obvious it was insulting. From behind

her he snorted loudly, and waited. When neither said anything to this, he asked, "When will you reveal yourselves?"

Adam stopped paddling again and turned painfully around to look at him, peering over his sunglasses. The canoe wobbled with this awkwardness.

In a tone that was almost convincing, Eden whispered shakily, "Martin? I'm a little scared ..."

It wasn't the use of "Adam's" real name that made him act, it was the sudden appearance of the duckling, which surfaced not far to the right of the canoe, instantly followed by a full-grown loon, which surfaced perhaps five feet away from it, quickly closed the distance and attacked with what would have been a lethal peck, had it connected. The duckling, which looked tired, shaggy and damaged from other pecks, dived again, and then so did the loon.

It was all he needed. She wasn't wearing a life jacket, so he had to get Adam, Martin, first. It was hard finding leverage while sitting, but as best he could he swung the paddle blade over Eden, or whatever her name was, and clipped Adam, Martin, just above the ear. It sounded and felt solid, but Adam, Martin, only hunched down into a ball, still conscious, clutching both hands to his head, his paddle dropped, drifting. Eden screamed words of some sort and, as if it were possible, lurched at both him and Adam at the same time, torn. He stood, balancing frantically with knees bent, and took another swing at Adam's, Martin's, head. The paddle blade caught the air like a wing, or maybe it hit something unseen, for at killing speed it lifted and missed his skull by an inch.

This swing toppled them. The water was nonsensically icy and he thought, Of course, they were high in the mountains. He felt his breath come in gasps, watched his body breaststroke toward the mouth of the channel into the reeds. He could hear her screaming, and a moan from her partner in answer.

He smiled at their surprise, whoever they were. He'd done well, as well as could be expected, but things might get ragged now. The pure and necessary always fell to the ragged and confusing. He neared the channel mouth and slowed his stroke; there was no way she would come after him, no matter how powerful a swimmer she might be. If she did follow him, into these reeds, it would be incredible, it would be fantastic— not only proof that this was all ordained, but also the most powerful choreography he'd ever been invited into. But she no longer felt a part of it.

Despite the life jacket it was hard going, partly because his dress shoes were useless for swimming. Breaststroking and breathing hard, he finally made the channel. He touched a foot down, could stand if he wanted to. He knew by her periodic screams that she hadn't followed. He let his feet settle into what felt like mud. He sculled himself forward while walking, head and shoulders above the water. Remarkably, he hadn't thrown his back out. He'd lost his hat but still wore his sunglasses; he took them off to shake away the drips, then replaced them. The channel was close-walled with reeds, about ten feet wide and winding. He turned the first corner. Her screams stopped. Perhaps a boat had arrived to help them. On the reedy bank not three feet from his face a big turtle startled at his approach and plunged in, and because the thing had launched itself in his direction, the absurd image arose of the turtle attacking him underwater, and it was real enough that he held his breath and tensed for it. When it didn't happen, he understood that he had just absorbed something of its power.

His walking breaststroke took him around one bend, then another. He could hear only the soft trickle of water against his neck. Above him, the sky's silence was pregnant. The sun remained hot, stern and instructive. He was still on course, a rightness he sensed but couldn't yet touch or see, up this remarkable channel, all the signs taking him to the spot where the light would shed its gauze, colours would deepen, and it would be revealed. There even seemed to be a slight current bearing him forward, and this could only be excellent. It was beginning to seem that all obstacles, perhaps years of them, had at last been overcome. He turned another bend. The green reeds, the water, the sky, his own body—none of them were barriers anymore. He could have sobbed with relief and gratitude.

Around another bend and, like God opening his arms, the reeds ended and the channel widened into a lake before him. He swallowed a guffaw and, shoes leaving the bottom, stroked into this new lake, letting it take him in, a pull of surrender. It was warmer in this smaller lake, the water silky and touching him everywhere, the genius of a quick and loving woman. Then he saw it. His breath caught, his throat thickened with growing joy. It took the form of a cabin, not thirty yards to the right, the only thing built on the whole lakeshore. A square float protruded out into the lake like a patio into a lawn. On the float, in sturdy wooden chairs, sat three. A trinity. They were in the form of women in their sixties. They looked to be drinking from elegant wine glasses. He could hear their warm, knowing laughter as they discussed him, a music he knew he would hear only this once.

The water was so calm he could swim with mouth just underwater and nostrils just above. He was close. The one with her back to him threw up her hand in a wave. He wondered if they had expected him to come from the water. He wondered what he would look like to them. His sunglasses, his frog-kicking feet bound in dress shoes. Nostrils skimming the surface. He couldn't help laughing. He was just twenty feet away, blowing bubbles of laughter and moaning out his nose, and they were pretending not to see him yet.

Cake's
Chicken

I've seen two things science can't explain. The first, I was fifteen and in the back seat of the family car, my parents in front. We were turning onto our suburban street, and I remember the light had that rich, early evening quality. Then, so fast we could only flinch, from the other direction a glowing ball shot by at speed, maybe head-high, missing us by mere feet. About volleyball-sized, glowing with the brightness of fire, or the orange of reflected sun, it had a metallic sheen, the gloss of a liquid bubble. It flew soundlessly, following the dips and turns of the street. That's how it was exactly. All three of us yelped and turned to it, but it was gone. We shouted versions of *"What the hell was that?"* and tried describing it to each other in amazed babble, but surprisingly soon my mother started talking fast about something else entirely, her way of coping with things she couldn't accept and would deny to her grave. My father eventually drank it away—when I mentioned it only a decade later he didn't know what I was talking about.

But I remember it exactly, as I do the second one, Cake's chicken. I still can't explain what happened that night I turned twenty-one, a while ago now. Sometimes the word "shaman" brings it to mind, and you hear that word more these days. I hear it and wonder if a shaman always knows he's a shaman. Or if he's necessarily good-hearted, or even smart. I wonder if shamans—or anyone who can work your mind like a tool—are confined to the hot southern lands or are scattered up here too, shamans unfocused and vaguely nasty, shamans masturbating at computers, shamans delivering your pizza, taking your tip with a deliberate stare.

Once I heard a social worker say she'd met "Rasputin in a group home," and I wonder if a version of that is maybe what I saw.

Because they weren't the brightest lights, Danny and Cake. In my last year of high school, I remember being attracted to their clique of two. I was a loner, still am, and I was probably drawn by their friendship, the friendship they had for each other, ugly as it was. Danny was tall, a jock without a team, a guy who maybe could have done okay in school if he'd cared. He was wry and acidic before irony became the norm. When he smiled, his eyes didn't, and he was hard to like. As for his buddy, if Cake was smart he hid it well. He was big too but sloppier, with a gut. I assumed he was called Cake because of that, but then I learned his last name was Baker, so who knows. Cake didn't seem to care about his nickname, or anything else. He "liked to have a good time," he said, which is maybe odd because I don't recall once ever seeing him laugh. He looked vaguely Asian, or maybe Mexican, and even slightly retarded, which is the word we used then. Rumour said he got violent without much reason. Probably I liked them because "not giving a shit about anything" looked like a bona fide wisdom you couldn't quite do yourself. Anyway, whatever magnetism worked then wouldn't now. Cake's dead and I don't like where Danny ended up.

I didn't see them for a couple of years, until I was in second-year university and starting part time at SuperSlice. They'd both been working at the takeout pizzeria "way too long," Cake informed me one evening in spring when we were doing the same three-man shift—one driver, one cook, one on phone and cash. It was a tiny place, always pounding hot, and Cake smelled bad as he rolled out dough, so I was wishing it was me, not Danny, on delivery. Also, Cake was the kind who worked hard in spurts to get it done, and I didn't like seeing the occasional drop of sweat course down his patchy unshaven cheek, bead on his chin, wobble and fall onto his work. But we were having a conversation, and it turned intense. He'd been going on about a problem he'd had with his health insurance since he'd turned twenty-one. Then he learned I was turning twenty-one that next Saturday and had no plans whatsoever.

"That's just bad." He'd stopped swirling sauce on a pizza to stare at me. He had the kind of thick straw hair that could never look good.

"No big deal," I said.

"You're turning twenty-one."

"Yeah, well."

"Your twenty-first."

Maybe he dwelled in some kind of American-movie fantasy. The drinking age here had been nineteen for decades. You could vote at nineteen. You could join the army and shoot people. Twenty-one was meaningless.

"Gotta do something."

"Maybe I will."

"This is the *twenty-one* twenty-one."

The two-speak was something I remembered from high school. They'd say, "You have to get her something. She's your *mother* mother."

"So let's do something." Cake had both hands up in fists, one of which gripped the wooden spoon. Tomato sauce dribbled onto his wrist. From this angle I could see that the scabbed cut on his earlobe was indeed what I'd hoped it wasn't—damage done by an earring ripped out.

"*Do* something with us."

"Maybe I should," I said. I admit I felt some yearning.

Cake said he and Danny were doing their annual camping trip next weekend, and I was coming. Bring a girlfriend or not, don't mind ours, he said. Trying to deflect, I asked where and he said the Cowichan River, it was a sweet spot, not an actual campground but a clearing at river's edge, a huge fire pit, a "homemade" picnic table. There was even a shitter made of an old chair with a circle cut out.

I mumbled how nice that all sounded.

His eyebrows were lazily up and his gaze steady. I didn't like looking him in the eyes. They were moist, and surrounded by pools of incomprehension and hurt, but they hooked and held you with a steadiness you didn't expect.

My stomach hollowed. Why was I scared? They weren't criminals, exactly. They probably did this sort of thing all the time, and apparently they survived. But I pictured smashed bottles and roars in the night, facial cuts, river-sized regret.

"I'm not much of a drinker."

Cake pursed his lips for a fart sound that could have meant a number of things.

THE FOLLOWING SATURDAY afternoon I was in my basement suite, trying out a rice cooker I'd bought at a garage sale and feeling fine to be turning twenty-one alone. My mother, maybe the only other person who knew what day it was, had called from Winnipeg.

But around five, the tiny red SuperSlice car pulled into the driveway. It sat a moment then honked, not sanctioned delivery behaviour. All I could see from my kitchen's little window was the car's grille and bumper, not the driver. I didn't know the eating habits of my middle-aged landlady upstairs, but I was apprehensive, and when another honk came, a long one, I ran outside to intercept Danny swearing to himself as he climbed the steps to bang on the main door.

"Danny!" I called, my hand up in a wave.

"Jesus, let's go, it's late," he said, not pleased. He was bare-chested, with his red SuperSlice shirt balled up in a fist. There sat Cake in the front seat, red shirt on, not looking at me, head bobbing lightly to music, eating a slice he'd folded up New York–style.

Danny brushed past me and in through the gate, muttering about "getting your stupid *stuff.*" I followed him into my apartment, where he stood in the kitchen, arms raised in the air, eyes closed.

"What are you bringing?" he hissed.

"I guess … I guess some blankets. We camping?"

"Yes, we're camping, and we have to *shop*, we have to buy *booze*, we have to *drive* and we have to set up a fucking *tent*. You were supposed to be at the Slice."

I called "Sorry" from the bedroom. I emerged with my duvet and pillow, both of which I stuffed into a garbage bag.

"I don't have a tent or anything."

Danny ignored me, watching the rice cooker.

"That done?"

"It needs a little m— The timer, I think, says fifteen—"

Danny unplugged it, wrapped it in his red shirt and tucked it under his arm.

"It'll keep steaming," he said. "It'll be good."

I told him it was brown rice, which made him halt and close his eyes again, but I couldn't tell if he was just being funny.

The hour-and-a-half drive began with a fight Cake and Danny had in the liquor store when Cake merely picked up some vodka and read the label.

"You don't want that," Danny told him.

"I don't know what I want," Cake said.

"Do I need to *list* why you don't want that?"

"Fuck you." Cake flipped the bottle to read the back, as if it were vintage wine.

"You're drinking beer. Throbhead here"—I was Throbhead, apparently because I'd continued in school—"can drink what he wants. I hope he buys something pretty fast, because we have a fucking tent to set up." Danny still wasn't looking at me. He was angry again because a store clerk had made him go back out and put a shirt on, and now his red shirt was wet and hot and smelled of brown rice.

I bought the best bottle of wine I could find with a screw-top, because of course I lacked a corkscrew. Danny bought a bottle of rum. I was perversely a bit disappointed when Cake settled on a six-pack of light beer, but things intensified in the car when, driving, Dan cracked his rum and began some steady sipping. When I asked why Cake wasn't driving, "He hates driving" was the answer I got, in a voice closed to any more comment. We were about ten miles down the highway before it occurred to me that these two guys were still on shift and stealing the SuperSlice's lone delivery vehicle to go camping.

Neither the car nor I would survive this, I knew. In the back seat, half-covered in torn sleeping bags and a crusty tarp, I wondered if this stuff would, or wouldn't, help with the fire and disfigurement when the crash came. I asked, casually enough, "So did work get another car or something?"

They were silent awhile, then Cake said only, "We been working there way too long. Almost four months."

"It was a *job* job," Danny whispered, mostly to himself, and he took a bluntly contemplative sip of rum.

Apropos of nothing, Cake told Danny that today was my birthday.

"Ohhh!" Danny said, as if this explained absolutely everything, and he found me in his rear-view mirror and gave me a grin and eagerly nodding head. When Cake added that it was my twenty-first, Dan bellowed and awkwardly thrust his bottle back to me, the car swerving as he did. I took it from him quickly. Not just to save our lives but to anesthetize what might be coming. Swallowing, I told myself it was just distilled sugar, Hell's candy, and what the fuck.

BUT IT TURNED OUT they weren't heavy drinkers at all. Danny pretty much stopped drinking once he stopped driving. At the campsite, Cake sipped listlessly on a single warm beer. I was also surprised that no bag of green came out, or pills—at least not that I saw. Basically, like two giant children, they had a natural and unfuelled capacity for mischief and discontent.

After we parked at the end of a dirt road we had to hike in a half mile along the river, so it was good we hadn't brought much to carry. Danny got the tent up with a dexterous ease that had Cake merely watching from the sidelines, passing him the next pole or peg. Or sometimes not. Their style took the route of obnoxious sniping—Danny's *"That* one, asshole," would have Cake fake throw it at him, and then toss it, cackling, out of reach—like boys half their age.

I did firewood, which was easy, hunting in the river-bank bushes for what looked like scatter from a flood, lots of nice-sized chunks there for the grabbing. Kindling had hung up in low branches, which was a good thing since we lacked a hatchet, or even a knife. The tent was crisp and clean, looking fresh from the box save for a burn hole on the roof the size and shape of a hot frying pan bottom. Someone had adorned the hole with magic-markered eyes and smile, so that the hole was a giant nose. The poorly drawn smile smoked a well-drawn pipe.

I'd finished building my base of balled paper, tepee of kindling and medium sticks girdering that, with a little wick of paper poking out in wait of a match. Danny walked past, widened his eyes as if in awe and then snorted. I was tempted to kick it down, join the sandbox mentality. I had them figured out now. These two were childish and fretful and competitive with nothing at stake, mostly just irritating, and this was the reason for their clique of just two. I lit the fire, twisted open my wine and tried to drink from the bottle with dignity. I was going to relax and enjoy my birthday. I would drink and have a good time despite them. I'd drink and have their good time for them.

The fire was having trouble so I knelt to blow into its smouldering base. Cake shouted from the riverbank, calling my name, then again louder. Eyeing my almost-fire I edged away to join them. Cake and Danny stood there taking in the sunset. It was a good one, no question—a glorious wall of orange and purple, with little ruptures that looked like balconies, from which shot rays of sacred light, behind which God made vast, heart-breaking decisions. Because they were so still, I glanced at the two friends' faces. Cake's expression was complex, for once. He seemed chastised by the sunset, humbled. But in his look there was also hope that what it was telling him might be wrong. Anyway, that's what I imagined I saw. As for Danny, his take on the beauty was simpler—he sneered. He was basically daring it.

We returned to my fire, which flickered perfectly. We took spots on the encircling logs as its audience. I saw there would not be much else to do here. I offered my wine bottle to Cake, who shook his head but grabbed and popped open another beer, though only for my sake, because I never saw him take a drink. Danny took a cosmetic sip of his rum.

As darkness took over, awkwardness grew around the fire. Not only was there no guffawing, no snapping of cans, but this campfire lacked the meditative stare that took art or wisdom from the embers. Mostly it felt like a raw kind of *pause*, broken by occasional mumbles. Cake flicked twigs into the flames, and Danny stood toeing the dirt, looking at the river impatiently. No one had said anything but I wondered if they were waiting for those girlfriends. I doubted it. Shirtless, jittery Danny looked like he'd been dragged through a pipe, was angry from the experience and unwilling to talk about it. Cake looked more settled, the kind of body that could happily play the same video game for a year. At one point Danny spent some time sitting on a log, but he faced away from the fire. In a way they resembled a married couple used to each other's silence. They seemed sad. Or at work on an endless puzzle. They wanted something to be hugely better. They would've destroyed things to get that, but there was just too much to destroy, and where did you start?

I was into my own little reveries when Cake, who looked especially retarded in the firelight but had apparently just read my mind, turned to me and asked, "So you even *have* friends?" The question was completely judgmental and didn't expect an answer.

I'd just been invited into their nasty little team, though I didn't know it at the time. It felt only sideways, a challenge.

"Never," I said, a kind of joke. Then added, macho, "Only girlfriends."

I was over being nervous with these two, and it wasn't just the wine. I was bored. Cake didn't respond, so I asked him, hadn't he said something about girlfriends?

"Never know, eh?" he said, inscrutable, gazing at the fire.

Danny snorted. Which made Cake shake his head.

Smiling falsely, I asked, "What?" I'd just suffered a sudden vision of a grotesque gay come-on, some really ugly bullying.

But Cake threw a twig at Danny, who let it hit his cheek. "We're thinking maybe mine likes him more. And also they hate each other."

Danny added, "*And* they lack a car. *And* they don't know where the fuck we even are."

"Doesn't look good," said Cake.

"Not for romance, anyway."

I threw in, "Nope."

Cake said, "I don't think they're exactly even a girlfriend …"

Considering this, Danny mumbled something about the larger scheme of things, and then said, louder, with a mirthless smile, "Talk about getting all worked up over nothing."

"So let's go"—Cake threw a bigger twig this time, which Danny dodged—"grab something to eat."

Danny closed his eyes and swore but got up anyway. He pulled on his red T-shirt and grabbed a flashlight, its beam so dim it was next to useless.

They disappeared down a near-invisible trail heading inland from the river. I hustled after them, following their noise, the moon barely showing me the trail. When I caught up, Danny said without turning around, "We got a chicken here last year. A huge one."

I fell back a few paces. There was no store for miles. Even if there was, it was probably midnight. We were about to have the kind of adventure I didn't want.

As if to taunt me, Cake said, "Me hungry."

"I am made of hunger," added Danny.

There was a pause where I was supposed to offer a stupid something of my own. I said I wasn't all that hungry, really, and that I totally could go either way. One last pull on my wine bottle emptied it. I let it drop on the trail.

CAKE TURNED OFF the flashlight when we reached a main path, a chip trail from the feel of it, and a farmhouse wasn't more than a hundred yards farther along. At our approach a dog barked but then, strangely, stopped. We stayed in the shadow of the woods as we made our way around a small fenced field. In the air the pissy sting of manure. Cake was lifting the wooden latch of a crude gate. I found myself tagging along with them. I didn't want to be ridiculed for hanging back, afraid. I had also decided that it was indeed my twenty-first birthday.

Walking in mud we made it to the back of a large, window-less shed that stank of something uniquely sour. Its door had the gate's same crude wooden latch, which Danny lifted. We all three crept in, Danny flicked on the weak light, and a shed full of roosting chickens, rows and rows of them, looked at us, clucking what sounded like frightened questions—then they all went crazy when Cake lurched and got one by the neck. They screamed, flapped, ran, fell, and though chickens supposedly can't fly, a dozen charged blindly into the ceiling and our faces.

Cake was trying to break the thing's neck right there in the shed, but Danny grabbed his shirt and pulled. A floodlight came on as soon as we left the shelter of the shed. It was hard to look at, so we must have been lit up bright. Cake had trouble running with the bird flapping against his direction, a kind of hysterical umbrella. He stopped to try a new grip on the neck. The chickens were still screaming. At the house a door banged open and after taking in our fleeing threesome a man spoke casually, it seemed, to someone inside. His voice was scarier than if he'd been yelling, because it sounded like the voice of someone who'd easily catch up and run beside us on the trail without us knowing it, and then when he killed us, one by one, he wouldn't talk at all.

TO MAKE SURE we hadn't been followed, we hid in the woods for maybe fifteen minutes and watched our dwindling fire from afar. It was an eerie sight, a minimalist painting about something interrupted or wrong: empty clearing, lone tent with a round hole in its roof, single full beer balanced on a log. I was glad I couldn't see Cake finally kill the bird; the noises were bad enough. I knew he'd swung the chicken baseball bat–style, trying to hit its head on trees. From the sounds, I think what worked was him simply holding it down and stomping. He may have tried biting it, because later at the fire a few feathers clung to his cheek, and Danny mumbled something about Ozzy Osbourne.

I took a big slug of Danny's rum, and another, then worked at getting the fire back to a blaze. We'd had time to catch our breath and settle down. Cake was quiet as he sat with his forearms on his knees, the dead chicken resting in his hands. When the fire hit its peak, he simply tossed the chicken in. Doing so, he said, "Last year was disgusting. This'll be better."

The feathers that touched flame shrank instantly brown, then black, smoke billowed, and a stink came at us. I didn't want to know what last year was like. Danny asked me if I had any of that wine left, and I took it for a fine-dining quip and didn't answer. I watched as the beak opened on its own. Then it gaped impossibly. The one eye I could see was sizzling. Smoke came off the head darker, a reddish brown.

"We should flip it," said Cake. The wings had almost burned off, but the mound of belly or chest that had ridden above the flame was still white.

Danny grunted but didn't move. He looked ready to sleep.

The two policemen were so quiet on their feet, they were suddenly just *there*, standing at the fire.

Danny jerked back and hissed, *"Jesus."*

"Morning, gentlemen," said one.

"Hiya doin'," said Danny. I grunted something through a squeezed throat. Cake was silent. Those little white fucking feathers on his cheek.

They were identically tall. They even looked a bit alike. Their uniforms seemed suited to a campsite, like park rangers or Boy Scouts or security guards—any brotherhood that keeps tabs on the wild. It was like they emitted the opposite of smell. They looked humourless and tired.

"You boys know anything about some chickens?"

No one spoke. The cops stood staring right into the fire at a bird that smoked and stank. They both carried head-bashing flashlights maybe two feet long. The timing grotesque, the sizzling eye went *pip* and now was an empty black smoking socket.

"Nothin' much," said Danny.

"Seen any kids running around?"

"Nobody."

I closed my eyes and shook my head. At the time, I didn't know that I was seeing the second thing science could not explain.

"Pretty quiet night, then," said the same cop.

Danny said, "Wanna warm light beer?" Smiling hopefully, he flicked a finger at Cake's three remaining beer, still in their plastic rings.

Mumbling "No thanks" under his breath, a cop found the beer cans with his flashlight beam. He aimed it to hunt in the shadows at our feet, then back to illuminate the open door of the tent, and finally shone it into the fire, right at the chicken. He let the light linger on it, and I swear I could feel his loathing.

"Okay, then," said the cop. "Have a good one."

The other cop flicked on his light and they both turned away. But as they did, the first cop swung back and shone his light full in my face.

"How old are you?"

I squinted and looked down. I've always looked young for my years. It was late, I'd had gollops more rum and I actually stumbled on the question, but before I could answer, Cake chirped, brightening because he had occasion to remember again, "He's twenty-one today! Yesterday!" As he grinned at them, a feather fell off his cheek.

The two cops disappeared up the hidden trail toward the farm.

"Gotta fucking flip it," Cake said, standing up. "Need a stick."

We could hear him stumbling around on the river gravel, swearing. He snapped a branch.

I asked Danny what the hell had just happened.

Staring into the fire, Danny yelled at Cake, *"What'd they see?"*

Cake yelled back, *"Pillow."*

Danny said to me, "They saw a burned pillow, I think."

"What?"

"He can do that. Make you see stuff. He has to be angry. Or nervous or something, *I* don't fucking know."

Cake walked into the firelight. "Grammy's ratty old couch cushion."

"What?" Laughing, I looked back and forth at the two of them. They seemed serious. "No way."

Cake said to Danny, "What they really won't see is the fucking car."

Danny looked skyward and whistled in relief.

"No way," I said again.

"He made the dog stop barking," Danny said. He turned to Cake. "Right?"

Cake murmured, "Whatever." He tried to flip the chicken with the stick, more a club. It kept falling back on its flat, burned side.

"Show me. Do it again," I said.

Cake fake lunged at me with a clawed hand. "Booga!"

I asked him seriously to prove it and he told me to fuck off. He applied himself again to the chicken, and got it to turn over and stay.

We watched the remaining white feathers burn.

"Isn't there something in there," Cake asked, almost rhetorically, jutting his chin at it, "a 'gizzard' or something? Suppose to be poisonous?"

Danny said if we found it we could eat around it.

PEOPLE HAVE TRIED explaining to me the science of the first one, the glowing sphere that shot past my parents' car, saying it had to be what's called ball lightning. When I tell them there wasn't a cloud in the sky, they look at me like they don't believe me now. Without clouds, their science is ruined and what I saw was impossible. But I know it wasn't lightning. It wasn't electric-white furious, it was a shining gold bubble. This second one, too, causes looks. People tell me the cops were obviously being ironic, wickedly straight-faced, asking about a stolen chicken even while staring at one, daring to share our crime in a way. Then laughing their heads off back in the squad car. But I saw their faces. It was the middle of the night and they'd hiked in to find nothing—no chicken, no dope, no booze to dump, not even noise to quell. They were sour bureaucrats. They saw a smouldering cushion and they hated the three miscreants who would defile a proper campfire by burning such a thing.

Anyway, I sat there on the log, and to my surprise I found I had grown hungry for the bird we'd cooked in the fire I'd built.

Eventually the black, charred thing got teased out with sticks and shoved onto a flat rock to cool.

What other explanation was there? Cake wasn't smart enough to be that good an actor; neither was Danny. And something in their boredom seemed to prove it all. So I'd just seen a guy use a wild power. One he maybe couldn't quite control. He just wasn't smart enough to do something bigger with it. To get a girl to see him as sexy. To make the world see things his way.

Danny didn't want his rum, so I kept drinking it, suffering the shudders that bring your shoulders to your ears. Though I didn't have it in words yet, I had learned a third unexplainable thing, which is that even if what we call magic is all around us, we'll never be able to prove it.

There they were, sitting in firelight, these two friends. Danny, twitching and distracted again already. Cake, pudgy, stupid and unreadable. But I saw now that—not even counting what Cake could do—these two were as rare as anyone. They were brave enough to steal cars and chickens, a route of wisdom I didn't have, and still don't. They took on sunsets.

Cake was mad because I kept staring. At one point my hair stood on end because of a sudden fancy—those weren't two cops at all. I'd been made to see cops. But I decided that was stupid—why make me see cops? Then, when I next looked at Cake, I saw a sort of bear-face instead of Cake, and at that point I just tried to forget the whole thing. And anyway it was time to eat the chicken.

We passed it around, all charred feathers and skin and the burned-off nubs of feet and head. Passing it, we got black to the wrists with greasy char. These two guys in their red SuperSlice shirts. I learned by watching them eat, and when my turn came I pulled at the black until some flesh followed, pieces of chicken that I recognized as parts of breast or thigh. Turning the hunk to my face, I used teeth and tongue to pull away pieces of perfectly delicious meat.

Cake watched me. "*Chick*en chicken," he said, smiling wisely, cheeks greasy black, eyes reflecting the idiot fire.

Any Forest
Seen
from Orbit

I have been asked to "explain things." Can I say simply that I'm an animal, with urges? It's the only explanation, truly. I didn't plan anything. I didn't intend a massacre, as it were. But—as they say—when weapons exist, they will be et cetera. This time, a chainsaw. I'm glad more people weren't hurt.

Yes, her name was Juliet, hard as that is to believe. Though not overly pretty, she was as sexy as sexy gets, in my opinion, and I suggest in her opinion too, which of course added to the allure. There's something about a woman aware of her own pheromones—it's not unlike a queen watching you as she bathes in milk.

It wasn't her beauty but more her imperfections I found carnal—her smallish eyes hungry and her slightly bucking teeth pushing her lips a little apart, keeping everything *ready*, as it were. She seemed always on the green verge of ripeness. Her humour seemed part of it too, though I can't even begin to "explain" that. But what can we make of a sexy woman who meets an average-looking man standing filthy at her door with a shovel and, wide-eyed, singsongs, "And who have we here?"

Let me declare again how average I look. In the mixed

vegetation of humanity, I am a blade of grass in a scrubby field. In the war of looks—it's very much a war and you know it—I understand that I am fodder. It's hard to lose count of certain things, and I'll explain that exactly three times in my life I've been called a "twerp." So I suppose I resemble a "twerp." I'm small, my build is soft. My face deserves some sculpting and a thinner nose. Plus, I've come to realize there's fear in my eyes and I always glance away. But my looks are no excuse for how this went with Juliet. Nor will I use as an excuse the very basic fact that I have not had any other chances in life to plant my humble seed—I'll just hand you that earthy nugget on its twerpy platter, and leave it.

All I really need to say is: Juliet was a surprise.

There I stood at her door, with my shovel. Seeing her, I became aware of my jeans swollen with mud and grass clippings, my aroma of dog waste and chlorophyll. For protection I wore my work glasses, the big old aviator style, which these days possibly look demented. Good God, and they're tinted yellow. Nonetheless, after singing at me, Juliet held my eye, fiercely, as she called upstairs,

"Troy, the man's here."

He got the singsong too. I was instantly jealous.

THE REAL EXPLANATION? The roots of a beautiful seventy-foot deodara cedar grew for more than half a century until they breached the sewer line of the Prudhommes' house. The tree was there first, but it rarely has rights in these things.

I was excited by their call because they'd responded to

the "arborist" side of the ad I leave thumbtacked on message boards throughout the city, not the "lawn and garden care" side. Mostly, yes, I cut grass and rake leaves. Almost exclusively, in fact. Yardwork is fine; there is mulching to consider, and the tines of one's rake need thought. But it is to trees that I apply my art, and vision.

Because, a tree. In the presence of an unfamiliar, beautiful tree—and they are all beautiful—for some moments I am unable to speak while I make my examination. I know that what I do might look like fondling, but I need to hold and to stroke, to feel most of all the bark against my cheek and, yes, my throat. Texture is how a tree communicates! I know some find me odd, I know it costs me work. Anyway. That day, answering the Prudhommes' call, I was excited that they lived not in a wealthy part of town but on a street of modest bunga-lows. Rich people use arborists all the time, if only to be able to say, at the club, "My arborist says," just like their caterer or their pool-boy says. So I was heartened that regular people had called an arborist. Perhaps it signalled a trend.

I was shown the problem tree. Juliet stood by while I circumambulated her deodara, then went in for my initial brush with fingertips, and inner wrists. Deo was abrasive but patient. I stepped back, I gazed up. Her trunk bent four times on its journey skyward, each time with the jauntiness of a cocked hip. This cedar expressed her female essence not unlike a geisha in traditional pose: hips tilted one way, head tilted another; face down, demure; arms at dramatic angles, holding fans. Exactly that, but with twelve arms and coniferous fans. A tree confident but quiet about her beauty.

Watching me, Juliet joked, "Now I know what a tree-hugger is."

I couldn't look at her. "The plumber, he's sure it's this—? That damaged the—?"

"They stuck a camera down the toilet. It's too bad. It's my favourite tree."

I took another step back, another gaze up. To me all trees are equal, but this tree's gestures were on the obvious side and I could see why someone might favour it. A breeze came up, and Deo looked pleased with her many small movements.

"Shame it has to come down," said Juliet.

"*Down?*" My hand, I saw, had grabbed a low branch. I regained composure, cleared my throat. I explained to her my plans, then I picked up my shovel.

WHEN JULIET TOLD ME her husband taught English at a community college I was surprised. Troy Prudhomme had a habit of punchy speaking, not unPalinesque. He eventually did come outside and, watching me dig the hole, reached in to remove a loose stone that kept getting in the way of my shovel.

"Well lemme just grab that *outta* there for ya."

When I got near the choked and broken sewer line, as evidenced by a rising tang, he laughed and said, "Hey! Welcome to our shit!"

Prudhomme seemed wary of proper speech, and I wondered what he was afraid of. Perhaps being accused of liking poetry. He was de rigueur four days unshaven. The arms protruding from his T-shirt were thicker than needed to teach college English.

As I dug to Deo's rampaging roots, Troy answered his cell and with a friend discussed plans for the evening: "Well, we snag some beers and watch the 'Nucks lose. You pick the place."

Hearing those words, Juliet, fanless but hip-cocked, caught my eye and nodded frantically, minutely. Her eyes had a soulmate's shine and depth as they yelled to me, *Tonight! At last! At last!* I'd been there all of twenty minutes. Less than that. I hadn't said a word to her. I am an average-looking man. Not even. Can I be blamed for anything?

In any case, I'd made a big hole. I'd reached the spot where root met pipe.

"Here we are," I said softly, stepping back.

Troy inclined his head as if to peer over a rim but kept talking into his phone about the 'Nucks and which players might play. He glanced at me, appeared to recall why I was there and turned to go inside. Juliet followed but spun round at the door and mouthed, ferociously, *"Ten after seven."*

And then, good God, she *pointed.* Not at me. Not at the ground beneath her feet. No, she pointed at her*self.* Below the belt. She pointed at the prize, while announcing the time it could be claimed. I'd never seen a human do that. I understand now that it is something an animal might do, if it had fingers, and could tell time.

To explain: my Juliet was pure.

I'VE BEEN IN DEEP FOREST and returned to the same spot after the trees were clear-cut. There is something, one thing, good about a clear-cut. It's there in the word. When all the trees are down, suddenly there is clarity. Sky. I don't know why a sudden sky is a good thing; why a revelation of distance, of clear space, is better than the dark complexity of a forest. Standing in a clear-cut is sad but it also feels like *relief* of a sort. Maybe it's because a natural riot of plants is so difficult. It's all branches and tendrils and thirst and an urge that can and will break through concrete. Who can walk a wild forest and not feel the threat of an unfathomable presence that parades as stillness? Plus, plants ultimately don't care about us. In the end, basic rock and sky is simpler to deal with, if we need to get spiritual about this, which I think we do.

The point I'm trying to make is, what we automatically think of as bad—for instance, a clear-cut—might actually be good.

I suffered such thoughts when I got home and stood under the shower. To put it plainly, I'd never been bad. Never. Not in that way. Of course I'd harboured the fantasies of any man whose job takes him from house to house, some of which, even in these times, contain lonely women. But I'd never taken advantage. To tell the truth, I'd never had the chance.

Was it wrong to have the chance? If I were to visit Juliet at *ten after seven*, was it any more evil than a tree letting a breeze take its pollen? Were wild oats *sin*ful?

Let me come out with it: I might, technically, have been a virgin. (Oh, I know it's a comic cliché, the older virgin, but there are more of us than you might think. In this war of appearance, many never do prevail.) Of my sparse adolescent fumblings, one involved alcohol and a cousin and seed was spilled, but I'm not sure exactly where or if it counted. If Anyone's counting, that is. And if no One's counting, can there be sin? It was a long and fundamental shower I was taking.

Juliet was beautiful beyond my dreams for myself, and such women are *naturally* out of bounds. I had decided not to go, yet I found myself showering purposefully, double-soaping crevices. I shaved a suspicious second time that day, then found myself eyeing my modest row of clean shirts, all tending to shades of brown.

I pitied my face in the mirror. More than once I've been called a hobbit, the attitude of the speaker being that I shouldn't be insulted by it. This was maybe my only chance. Can it even be right to never do wrong? Can light exist without dark?

It was time for my root to break pipe, as it were.

AT A QUARTER PAST SEVEN I strode up the drive, taking note of the missing Troy-car. I feigned confidence by pretending to be here not for Juliet but for the offending deodara cedar. I positioned myself over the hole and, breathing shallowly, because it did smell of sewage, gazed in for a meditation on roots. There they were, exposed in all their bulbous, knuckled glory. In two places, root fist had crushed ceramic neck of sewer line, during a fight utterly dark and slow. A bigger root moved under the pipe, missing it. It could stay. But these two would have to go. The tree would be injured. Half of Deo might yellow and die, but she could be trimmed, shaped. I had told the Prudhommes my plan. A half tree can be lovely. One can mould its weakness not unlike a bonsai. Giant art. Hunchbacked, leaning, it would still be beautiful. How could it not?

I stood at the hole. The door opened and didn't close, and Juliet came up quietly.

"Troy," she said, shyly pressing a shoulder into mine, "wants it taken down."

"He wants it taken down," I repeated, to make sure I'd heard right.

Here in this rainy, verdant city, the popular way with any problem was the chainsaw. No one wanted the care involved in nursing a tree back to health. Cut it down, dig out the hole, stick an expensive foreign sapling in.

"I'll—I'll do all the follow-up. The shaping. For free. Everything."

"He wants it gone. He already phoned somebody. He didn't like you."

"That's—nothing but a shame," I said, meaning it, forgetting for a moment why I was here. "What do *you* think?"

"I think we should go inside. I mean, it smells *great* and everything, but ..."

I find not unsexy those women who own up to their own dirt, as it were. Not throw it crassly in your face, but smile in admitting they do indeed poop. And the poop goes down that pipe and onward to the sea, there to fertilize languid seaweed that sways, unseen.

I DON'T KNOW IF JULIET was like this only with me. Maybe she'd seen the way I touched Deo? And wanted some of that for herself? The thing is, she asked me to brush her hair. All of it, everywhere.

Juliet Prudhomme shaved nothing on her body. Her hair was a tawny-blonde and there wasn't that much of it. The hair on her legs was the same as on her forearms, in that you had to concentrate even to see it. In her armpits nested two cute tufts. I sensed the depth of her strangeness only when she undid the piled hair on her head and it cascaded down her back, uncut, certainly, for years and years. I could hardly breathe, let alone hold a brush, but I did what she asked. I brushed, shaking all the while, hoping she'd take my hand's tremor to be a little extra something I brought to my erotic art.

There in her bedroom, husband Troy at some bar, Juliet sat on the edge of her bed and I knelt, in only my boxer shorts, brushing her long, beautiful hair. She'd lift an arm and I'd draw the brush, once, twice, through her pit, the tines softly tugging through. When I did her legs she parted her knees so I could reach the insides of her thighs, and I encountered the vision I was born to behold. There, eye level, was the crux of my adventure and the spot at which she'd pointed. Edging out past a hem of pearl silk underwear was her humble rim of vulva, mounding demurely, in the sense that it couldn't help but mound. It too was graced with a fine, squirrel-blonde hair, also awaiting my brush. I could not think and my breathing was ragged. I don't know why, as I have limited experience in these matters, but her fine hair—its slight lustre, the arc of its uniform wave— suggested the essence, the *soul*, of Juliet. It was both how and what she communicated. I saw this and believed it as much as I would have the main thrust of a philosophy, had I one.

I'll say nothing more. I've described enough. Goodness knows I've described the brushing, and what followed, over and over in my head. As I review this cycle of images it's like I'm strapped to a paddlewheel: I'm plunged under and come up drenched and choking but I can't wait to go under again. It's my private memory and it will last me my lifetime.

I was like a plant responding irresistibly to the sun, but at human speed. Picture, if you must, a gnomish man embracing utter beauty, clenching it with hands, legs, wrists, mouth—and leave it at that. Because the embrace, the fecund exchange, did take place. Twice, at my eager plea. After the second time, Juliet told me to be still as she listened carefully to the radio she'd brought into the bedroom so she could hear how much time was left in the hockey game. It would be over in ten minutes.

So she turned to me as I lay smug (I'm thinking now) on my pillow, and said something.

In our short time together she'd said other things too, of course. Before, during and after our embraces. She said I was "sweet," and several times called me "sweetie." After I'd performed a certain little something with my fingertips, moving them on her bum-skin as on the breakable membrane of a mushroom, she told me, "You're great at that." Once she pressed my nose with her thumb, one of her little surprises that kept me reeling, that dug an instant hole under me and made me fall even further in love.

In love. There it is. In my life I have had almost no chance to give myself like that. To give my body. To bloom, as we were meant to. I have this body *in order for it to bloom*. Juliet!

Then she said that final thing. After checking her clock radio, then meeting my eye as inconsequentially as she would a passerby's on a rush-hour sidewalk:

"So that was all great, but now you have to get out. Don't ever come back."

I watched Juliet's face for a smile. None came. It wasn't humour.

THE NEXT MORNING I sat rooted in shock. After getting home I'd actually fallen asleep and slept fully. A drained husk, as it were. I woke with the birds and felt replenished, richly spunky again. Potent with confusion. I couldn't get her words out of my head. I counted them all, many times. The woman I loved had uttered either seventy-six or seventy-seven words to me, including the urgently mouthed *"Ten after seven"* at her front door. I did not count her pointing finger, her inconceivable jab at herself. How many words did that signal represent? How many theories? Books of philosophy?

I can explain that I wasn't seeing clearly. I felt bewildered— and now I see the perfection of that word. Lost in the wild! I cried and it made me feel better. Crying gave rise to all the possibilities, and their logic dried my tears. I saw that she might be in love with me too, and said what she *had* to say, painful as it was for her. Or, it could be that Troy was murderously jealous, and she said it to save my life, even while ruining hers.

I stood under a hopeful shower again. But whatever my thoughts, however they swirled, stroked or hit each other, I wasn't seeing clearly. How could I? And that's why what happened, happened.

To say that I almost didn't return to the Prudhommes', to my job with the deodara cedar, would be a lie. I am an arborist.

In other words, I had two precious reasons to return, even if, that morning, they felt like one.

LIKE ALL OUTDOOR tradesmen constrained by noise bylaws, I could arrive at my jobsite no earlier than five to nine. Troy had been busy on the phone, it seemed, because here was my competition climbing out of his bigger shiny white truck, "Petersen's Tree Service" in black Times Roman on the door, all the charm of a tax form. Under that, *Forty years in business*. I often saw Petersen's truck around town. It should have read, *Forty years destroying your trees without a moment's thought*. Petersen's monkey-boy sat in the passenger seat gulping coffee. He'd be scaling the tree to do the real work, topping the tree in sections and lowering them by rope to Petersen.

Petersen sat oiling a chainsaw on the truck's tailgate. He was big, and he had cut the sleeves from his shirt to reveal his formidable arms. But like many of the smaller species, I puff up when threatened. And perhaps my yellow aviators make me look capable of surprise.

"What's up?" I asked, trying at the same time to make my chainsaw look weightless in my hand, which means not letting it tilt me to one side.

"Not much." Petersen didn't even bother looking at me. Which told me that Troy Prudhomme had said something.

"This is my job here," I said. "The deodara. Gonna half-root it, heal it." I dropped the "g" not through fear but as a peace offering.

"Um, we're buckin' it. They called."

"When?"

"I don't know. Last night."

"That's impossible."

He looked at me blankly. I had one good lie ready. Old-growth activists use a tactic called "spiking," where they drive hidden nails randomly into a random tree. A man wielding a chainsaw can be killed. Spiking just a few trees and making it known can save whole forests.

"There's no way they'd call you. It's been *spiked*."

"No way."

I stood slowly nodding.

"Who the fuck spiked it?"

"She did. The wife. Juliet. I guess she's just absolutely in love with—"

"*She's* the fuckin one *called* me."

"Who called you?"

"She did. Mrs. Prudhomme."

"When?"

"*I* don't fuckin know."

"*When?*"

"I don't know, last night. Six? Said it was an emergency."

"*Six?*"

I stood staring past him, at Deo, seeing nothing and everything. This last piece of evidence about Juliet did a quick job of flushing all life from me. It's why I did what I did. It wasn't rage, per se, it was panic. It was a last-ditch attempt to save my world.

I yelled a fateful noise, I started my chainsaw. I didn't nick Petersen—that's a lie. My blade missed his face by two feet, or maybe one, but in any case he leapt back. Another leap put him in his truck, and I bet he nicked his own face on the way in. He jabbered to his monkey-boy as they sped away, the tailgate open and his chainsaw rattling and walking along its edge. The white truck gleamed in the sun as it turned a corner and was gone. I assume it was Petersen who called the police?

I don't remember going to the tree. To Deo, growling machine held in front of me. I do remember starting the cut because of the intense pleasure I took from her pain. And maybe, sure, maybe I was aiming the tree at the house. So in that sense it's true that I "used the tree as a weapon." But if you only knew how few trees I've taken down in my life—almost none—and how rudimentary my cutting skills are. I have, at best, a sense that a tree might fall north as opposed to south. The question shouldn't be "did I," but "could I."

I cut. Barely used, my machine roared when unleashed, the teeth of its blade pristine and eager. I breathed smoke as cream-yellow chips spewed against my legs and piled on my feet. Oh, the reek of cedar, the gorgeous, shrieking scent of its fresh blood, of its dying. Maybe the smell scraped my eyes, because I found I couldn't see through the tears. Her death took less than a minute, but in that time I could replay everything.

It was my Juliet who had called. My Juliet who, after our second embrace, had said to me, in bed, in slumbery amusement, "So, you really love that tree."

I'd been giving her my thoughts, that *seeing* a tree was to behold its heartbreaking relationship to the sun. It was like God and supplicant; it was a successful religion. I spouted the usual, the stuff I'm no longer so wild about.

"You think trees are so special," she said, six more words I thought she meant.

"More than that!" I exclaimed, obnoxious. I told her how blind we were to each plant's uniqueness, and that we should never call them by their species. "If we call that tree an oak, we'll see an 'oak,' not *the living process of that single being*."

"I thought it was a deo ... deodo ..."

"I'm using 'oak' as an example."

"Deodorant!" she said, not listening. She added, "Ironic," in that singsong of hers, and I suppose she meant her sewer being broken by a deodorant tree. But I was breathless with my theories and growing breathless for another reason too, wanting embrace number three.

My monstrous chainsaw roared its triumph. The second before Deo leaned, shouting her orgasmic final crack to begin her fall, Troy appeared on the cute little deck that issues from their bedroom. Had I aimed the tree at this bedroom? Who knows. You won't believe me, but I do think it was the tree's aim more than mine. Deo had been aiming herself all her life. So had I. So had Juliet, and Troy. It's why we love trees—we see ourselves in the rooted and the helpless.

Troy tried to catch Deo. It was so pathetic and hopeful a move that it made me like him. His arms raised to the sky were a cuckold's arms—that is, a lot like a child's. Twenty Troys couldn't have caught that tree's tons, twenty Troys couldn't have protected Juliet, who yet again lay languishing post-coitus in her bed, a bed she had shared with exactly one too many.

I'M TOLD JULIET'S in a coma. Am I sorry?

Troy, apparently, will walk again. Shoulders heal, as do vertebrae. He'll wear his facial scars proudly to English class and 'Nucks games. No, I'm not sorry. For I can say that I'm seeing more clearly now. I see, for instance, that Juliet is still in control. No, she's not faking her coma. She's not a possum. But I do know she's an animal, hiding and in wait.

I can see how I've changed. Though it might have come through in my explanation, you'll be surprised at the new me, especially when you hear me say: Any forest seen from orbit is a carpet of breeding mould. At war with absolutely everything. Trees are shit. Trees, *all* plants, are shit. They are teased up, *tortured* up, by the sun. They fight each other for its light, squeezing out what competition they can. Green *is* envy. Texture is defensive and mean. Do you know how many pretty garden plants exude poison through their roots, and gasses through their leaves, to keep weaker plants small, and in the shadows?

Do your worst to me. It's expected.

I sometimes feel like a mushroom, not just because it eschews the sun. And not because a mushroom is the hobbit of the plant world. Anyone can tell by their shape and colour that they bulb about in a blind and comic hell. Mushrooms are twerps. Some are dangerous. Good.

I could go on, but no more explanation is needed. Look at me. Now look at Juliet. Even in a hospital bed, Juliet has me beat. Even now she has someone in there tending her hair, as it were.

Tumpadabump

Chantal stops the taxi five blocks early, wanting to walk. Actually wanting not to walk, wanting this not to happen at all, this final dispersing of the will. She has not been this far downtown in months and she hates it. She believes she probably always has, the soulless glass towers and banal exhaust fumes. She wants home and its grand stone buildings, each as ripe with odd spirit as a human being; she wants the Seine's good stink.

But there is only today. With the doling out of Bill's assets, maybe he will exist a little less. Maybe this will help clear her head. Dr. Michel said that today's meeting "might unstick the glue. It might trip up the rhythm." Those were his words. Also, "Maybe he'll stop seeking your attention." Dr. Michel was a bit of a *caricature* getting her to come here today, excited and gesticulating to shoo her from his office, *Go! Go!*

She glances up to the green glass tower, stomach hollowing. Bill's son, Cameron, will be here. She has met him many times, including Christmas dinner twice. It was not terrible. She would watch him, civil in his upright posture, wrestling intelligently with himself, trying to get on with this Frenchwoman, only ten years older than him, this *salope* who had displaced his mother. But now here she is getting more money than him, much more, and even to her this feels not right. The condo she is fine with—it is her home. She is also getting the Porsche, which she has not yet driven. But then she is getting the insurance money, which for an accidental death is exactly one million dollars. Cameron gets two hundred and fifty thousand, *un peu excessif* for a twenty-four-year-old aimless kid, but nothing to replace a father, and not as much as she is getting, which is the point. She who came along and broke up a family, who was married to him a mere three years. And in their country not much longer than that. Cameron's mother is getting nothing. Bill composed the will and allowed no grey.

Today Chantal wants to tell him, she wants to say to Cameron that she did not expect this money. She wants to say how much she loved his father. She needs him to believe her grief. Mostly she wants to tell him—yes—how *bizarrely* Bill died. And explain that an emergency can be endless. That sound can become a parasite.

She reaches the building. In Paris they would have demonstrated against this green *atrocité*. Only two people have recognized her on her five-block walk. That quizzical stare— *Now, who … ?*—before they realize she is Metro's Meteorologist. "In the flesh" is the expression. Her apparently famous cheekbones. Her "European flair," whatever that is. She suspects it is just her accent. To find flair in imperfect speech is to infantilize, but so be it. She suspects accents are sexy in men because they suggest exotic knowledge, but in women they suggest vulnerability. It took her some months to learn how not to call him *Beel.* In any case, as Bill cheerfully pointed out, her career onscreen was going to have its superficiality. It does disturb her, being recognized. Though she always smiles back, for her career. She has not given up her dream of serious journalism, of anchoring, despite the bad signals she has had. Bill called these the ghosts of freedom fries.

She pushes through the tower's revolving door, a seemingly playful technology that unnerves her, but once through she enjoys the cool, cleaner air (Bill's "corporate air") of the atrium, its vast, alert space and the spatter of the gauche fountain. It does clear her head for a moment … then Bill comes back.

In fact they met here, at that party on the top floor. The concierge at the central desk offers his "Hello, Mrs. Robertson" with a sadly knowing tilt of the head. At first she thought it kind when Bill's colleagues insisted they take on his probate, assuring her they knew estate law, they were not just entertainment law, God no, they did that only because it was lucrative and, well, entertaining. Bill called it contract law, because that is what it was; they specialized in media, which meant music and films and television. At that party upstairs he said, "Weather Girl, meet Entertainment Lawyer. Nonsense, meet Oxymoron," even as they shook hands. She did not understand what he had said until later. By then she saw his endless cynicism, and how it was excused by all because he was just as cynical about himself.

The elevator is empty and Chantal presses the silly 14 that should be 13. At that same party Bill talked her out of becoming a "meteorologist," the label her station was adopting. Talked her out of it while seducing her at the same time. First he asked if they still said *vachement* all the time in France. She said not so much as her parents' generation had, a gentle dig at his age. Too bad, he said. I mean, it means "cow-size." It's the best expression I've ever heard. It's *vachement fou, non?* Then he told her she could not be a meteorologist. Everybody already knows the term is fake. That same stupid weatherman is suddenly a meteorologist? It's worse for you, he said. It's an insult. You're there reading the weather because you're exactly the person everybody wants to look at and wants to hear. You're there because you're perfect. He said this with a small shrug. Pretending you're a scientist is demeaning. Insist against it, he said, adding, It's cow-size stupid. He walked off with both their glasses to get them fresh drinks, assuming she had not had enough of him. She watched Bill go and watched him at the bar, wondering at his odd ugliness and large grace and if maybe he were gay. She found out when he came on to her ten minutes later, right after his twenty-second sketch of a dead marriage played out with his hands as if they were puppets. One of the hands was lying there dead and the other was humping all over it. Bill never smiled once. He did not care what you thought of him. No, that was not it—he would care deeply if you stopped liking him, but it would never make him change anything he said or did. He asked if she wanted to "take in some gourmet air" out on the balcony. When she saw his humble regard for the vista of city lights, which he seemed to find enigmatic and which of course was his only mystical firmament, she thought she could make this man content. And she was partly right. She did fight successfully against becoming a meteorologist for another two years. Her segment stayed, simply, "The Weather, with Chantal."

At number 14 she departs the elevator with her heart in her throat and a piano version of a Beatles song tinkling behind her. "Michelle," their French one. Bill once told her that elevator music was the true white heart of North American culture. She continues to hear too clearly so much of what he said to her.

And continues to hear him fall down and die.

SO SHE MUST UNDERSTAND HIM. It is funny that she does not know if he was *funny*. "Funny" being such a funny word. Maybe he was funny spelled w-e-i-r-d. Maybe she still does not know what funny is over here. Sometimes Bill's small remark would make everyone laugh except her, or sometimes she was the only one to laugh. Maybe it was a French *truc*. In fact he often could remind her of a Frenchman. An old, typically clear-headed yet twisted man, a philosopher in the way all old Frenchmen are, islands unto themselves and always right despite the ocean of evidence to the contrary. It is true, his irony could grate. Once he quoted to her, "Irony is the sound of a bird in love with its cage," an image so self-knowing it made her forgive everything. He was being ironic, of course.

But he *was* funny, not just morose, morbid, *mordant*. Once, soon after their new passions had cooled and *la différence* had relaxed, when he touched her elbow next to the bed and she told him she was so tired it would be like being with a dead fish, he paused as if considering, and asked, "Dead how long?"

She needs to understand exactly one thing about him. His jokes—if you could use that word—often appeared to surprise him too. They seemed to take him places, the way one might follow a sudden dark alley. All the while saying, *Look at me.* This was important too. She almost does not like to think of this. Not a month into their marriage, her cheek pressed to his shoulder, she watched him shaving and said something like, "*Mon dieu,* to have to shave your *face.*" At this, he stared harder into the mirror, growing clownishly bug-eyed as if discovering the gravitas of her comment even while scraping through foam. He proceeded to draw his razor in front of his ear, shaving off his entire sideburn as he did, and then still farther up, slow and hard so she could hear the cut bristles, dragging a new path, destroying his haircut and in the end having to shave his entire head. He does not act like a lawyer, she thought at the time; he violates laws of common sense. She wondered about his colleagues, these repressed arbiters of civilization, and came to see that lawyers often acted *le roi du flan* but were in fact frustrated about something deeply general. Many drank heavily as a controlled hobby. But Bill did not drink like that. He was neither repressed nor civilized. He was certainly not drunk when he died. He did not just fall down drunk.

She noticed his jealousy of clients. Bill would use the word "artist" facetiously, especially around young musicians. He was easiest to read here, his mockery so plain. Female singers sang "emo-porn," he said, and tough-voiced guys had their balls in their throat. No, *hairy* balls in their throat. The good-looking clients were "faces." (And might not that be me? she wanted to say.) By the time clients could afford his help they were rich, and in his view overnight spoiled brats. If they deigned to meet with him at all he was seen as "the bearer of mysterious numbers" as well as "a boss they could fire." Once he did get fired when word got back to a singer (a face) that in a meeting Bill had lifted and shaken a laptop while claiming that it could make *him* sound as good. He detested certain rappers especially, called them pigs, and he hated "doing their arithmetic." But he liked the theatre people. Chantal thinks she remembers him saying, "They seem to know they're crazy as babies."

But largely his clientele depressed him. Maybe it was because they were doing something creative while he was not. His colourful clients even seemed to make him regret his own name. Bill Robertson, a bland one.

What matters is the depression. How it fit, how it might fit, with humour. With joking. It is this that she needs to know.

CHANTAL PAUSES at the grand mahogany door. The corridor is perfectly silent, so his rhythm is insistent. She thinks she hears Cameron's laugh. It should relieve her, that his son might be at ease with all of this today, but it does not.

Chantal wants to ask Cameron something but knows she will not dare, because it will sound only horrible and she will not find the best words: *How far would your father go to tell a joke?* Another thing she will not ask him, less because it might risk the insurance money than because it might hurt him: *Do you think he was suicidal?* And, *If he did kill himself, he would make it funny, wouldn't he?* She can picture Cameron's face. He would think she was crazy. He would think her even crazier if she asked, *Why did he not love me enough to stay?*

Janet, one of the several secretaries, rises and gives her those huge, intimate eyes that were at first a balm to Chantal until she

saw how everyone got them and they were Janet's main talent
here. From the way Bill acted around her—a flirtatious man
with flirtations too chastely held in check—Chantal suspected
some history between them.

She is ushered into an anteroom and from his chair
Cameron looks up, and she sees she will be waiting here alone
with him. He lowers a *Sports Illustrated.* He looks uncomfortable, unsure if he has to talk or can keep reading. Bill bemoaned
their difficult relationship, describing his son as "judgmental,"
unaware of this pun on his profession, so afraid of his son was
he. Cameron closes the magazine, looks up at her again. With
the force of a shove she encounters Bill in the son's eyes. It is
all she has seen of Bill in these past eight months; it surprises
her and she wails, mouth open, staring at the son. He does not
get up. He is afraid. She hugs herself, fiercely, because someone
has to.

IT WAS NOT LIKE he had suddenly become more depressed. He
was not happy, no, but you could tell that he never had been.
In a way, unhappiness seemed to sustain him, not unlike one
of those hound-faced comedians who make a running joke out
of their troubles.

And it *could* have been the stroke that took him down. She
still tries to cling to this. He was not fit. Clothes off, he verged
on tubby. He returned from his last physical to tell her, smiling,
that he was not unhealthy but delightfully cumbersome, like
a stuffed animal. I have the body of an English judge, he
said once, eyebrows raised, like this might make some sense

to Chantal, who had lived in England for three years before coming across the ocean.

The autopsy determined a stroke, but one brought on by the fall and head trauma. She asked a doctor if the stroke could have come first, could have been why he fell in the first place. The doctor said probably not, but it was possible. So Bill might have had a stroke, *then* dropped into the bathtub, hitting his head. So it might have just been a coincidence. A coincidence *vachement bizarre.*

Because, this is what she has told no one:

They had been fighting again. Maybe this is key, maybe it is not. Bill was having a shower, the door ajar and the window open, because the fan needed repair. He enjoyed long, hot showers, standing swaddled in steam. She was in the living room reading and could hear the spray, the changes to its tone as he moved under it. She was reading *Wheat Belly.* After their fight she wanted to gently reveal its thesis to him, though this would more than likely make him come home with a cake that he would eat in front of her, in the end making her laugh. She thinks she remembers him singing or humming in the shower, but she cannot be sure, though it was something he would do—sing—during one of their silent fights. But he had not been drinking. Or taking any drugs. It was never drugs with him, except on occasion, and these he would report almost proudly to her, once when he had snorted a line, "a meaty rail," with a client, and other times when he "saw Tom Bombadil," which was his assessment of weed.

So he was sober. He was showering, and maybe singing. She heard something bang and bounce on the counter, then the floor. Even at the time she guessed correctly that it was an empty shampoo bottle thrown over the railing, blindly aimed at the waste bin. Perhaps as a first step toward seeking a truce, she called out, "Are you okay?"

"*What?*"

"Are you okay?"

"*Why?*"

"I thought maybe you slipped."

There was hardly a pause. Maybe there was no pause.

"*If I slipped it would sound like this.*"

Then, the unimaginable sound of Bill's body hitting the bathtub.

There were four tightly connected thuds, four syllables to the sound of his body contacting the coated steel. From the injuries you could tell what body part made a sound. One syllable was an elbow. Another his right shoulder. These were the two middle syllables. One was his general torso, his gut and chest and pelvis hitting the tub's bottom. That was the last syllable, muffled and deep. The first, the killing blow, was his head. That is how she construed it when she heard it again. For she could hear it, over and over. She had trouble deciding which was the loudest syllable; it was a case not of volume but of tone. Of *insistence*. Dr. Michel suggested that her ardent attention to the sound as it repeated itself in her head meant that she was trying to hear the instant of Bill's death. The sound that changed everything. But even hearing it the first time, she had understood what the horrible percussion was telling her. She knew his head fell the farthest. She knew his head hit first.

The four syllables took one second. Within this duration of sound she had been overwhelmed, Dr. Michel told her, and the sound had engraved itself. Which was why the sound would not stop. And why she could not sleep. And could not concentrate. Chantal found this odd, because was not concentration the opposite of falling asleep?

Even as the doctor was explaining all of this, the insistent four-syllable murmur fought with his voice, and she understood that she had been infected. She asked Dr. Michel if that sounded accurate, that she had been "infected" by a sound, and he considered, then nodded, and said it would not be inaccurate to see it this way. He added that it was not unlike a soldier's being infected with an image of a sudden and bloody explosion.

There were other images—why had they let her be? There was the sound of his breath after the fall. It was like a loud sigh, one admitting, "Well wasn't *that* stupid of me." But it was the last exhalation, the heralding of death's perfect peace—this she knew before she drew the curtain back. Sometimes she thought it *had* sounded like relief, a person's relief to finally be dead, and perhaps because of this the image was allowed to fade. As would the sudden smell as she drew the curtain—his bowels. As would the sight of him, face down, the off-kilter alignment of limbs that left no doubt.

There in Dr. Michel's office, Chantal was stricken by his agreement of "infected," and she panicked, speechless, leaping from her chair to flail her arms as if swimming through the gruesome rhythmic thumping. It was a claustrophobia and a torture one had never heard of. The non-stop sound of one's love, dying. Dr. Michel came round to take her shoulders and face her, his touch stopping the sound for a moment.

"Time," he said. As if to inoculate her with this truth, he squeezed her shoulders and repeated himself.

It has been eight months. Though it sometimes recedes in volume, the sound in its constant rhythm has become not smoother but instead more crude, and fierce, skin and bone and *spat*. In the way a repeated word loses meaning, this word gains it, though the meaning is something she cannot understand other than as one understands nausea. It has become a clownish word, an American-sounding word. Sometimes she is certain Bill is mocking her. It is never not there. Usually it is softly percussive, like her own breathing, but there are times when she cannot hear people talking to her. There are times at work when she reads the prompter and gestures with balletic hand the contour of the frontal system approaching from the west, and the sound follows her hand and grows in idiotic volume as if she were beckoning it from the bathroom.

She still does not know what any of it means. What does this infection *mean*?

ONE. BILL HAD A STROKE in the shower, then fell, hitting his head. This was *possible*, said the doctor. Making it far less possible was the detail they did not know, which was him announcing, "If I slipped it would sound like this," *then* having a stroke and falling. If this were the actual scenario, it would amount to a coincidence the size of which would prove that absurdity is the essential spirit of God.

Two. Bill said what he said, then launched himself. They were fighting and he did not care about *anything* except the blooming of an unimaginable joke. This lunatic scenario does unfortunately catch the soul of Bill. *Mort de rire.*

Three. Bill said what he said, and to create the sound he moved to pound the tub with a fist. In his eagerness to perform well, he slipped. But if he was already bent over close enough to the tub to pound it, how had his head fallen so fatally far?

Four. Bill said what he said, then decided to kill himself as the punchline to the best joke he had ever told. But dashing your head on porcelain, even from six feet up, is a very uncertain way of ending it all. Unless he was so instantly desperate to die that he did not consider the method.

Five. She did not know him at all. He was an awful magus who infected her, impregnated her with his last instant of vitality, in keeping with an ugly man eternally jealous about his beautiful wife.

Six. Bill envisioned everything. His joke-that-keeps-on-telling was his lawyer's knowledge that she could lose the insurance money if anyone caught even a whisper of numbers three through five. Or this one, six.

Seven. None of the above. She does not understand what happened.

CHANTAL HAS STOPPED crying and is embarrassed. She takes a seat two chairs from Cameron, whose face is not sympathetic, whose eyes are half-closed. She imagines this is the look he wears at any thought of her. He seems to have forgotten his magazine.

Of course there were suspicions, right from the start, about everything, as if all beauty-and-beast unions are sordid. Worst of all was her age, and this closeness to Cameron's. She is almost his contemporary, and he knows "what makes her tick," is the odd expression. She still hurts recalling the evening Bill "accidentally" left them alone for an hour and she tried her utmost to be friendly. She smiled overmuch, and yes, she touched his shoulder—it was a nice black-on-brown linen shirt—and his hard glance back denounced a *coquette*. She wonders if Cameron remembers that evening when he was over for dinner (trying to impress, she prepared *salade de canard confit*) and Bill seemingly insulted her. When she mentioned to Cameron her ambitions to be a TV news journalist Bill had snorted and under his breath mumbled, "Now *that's* an oxymoron," and while she understood that he had snorted at the oxymoron and not at her, she suspected that Cameron, smirking into his *salade*, heard only the snort, the apparent insult. She had been too shy, and proud, to speak up and fix things.

She notices now that Cameron has dressed up in good clothes for this, out of respect for his father. The charcoal sports coat looks new. His trousers are rumpled near the crease. As far as she knows, he still lives alone.

She wants to tell him that she can still hear his father, hear him hitting the tub. She wants to ask him if it is possible for something to be this *vachement coincidentale*.

Cameron, perfectly unmoving. The heavily lidded eyes. It

strikes her that maybe he is just sad. He is as inscrutable as his father. He exudes a familiar depth.

"Cameron. Can you please do me the favour of taking the car? Will you have the Porsche?"

He tilts his head, eyeing her, surprised. He speaks clearly and slowly.

"Wouldn't be *legal.*" He can mock a word like his father could.

"Please. A son should have his father's car."

"Well, some fathers don't think that way, I guess."

"No, it is mostly selfish of me to ask. You see, it will make me feel better, and I want to feel better."

This makes him look away, into the middle distance. His expression is impossible to read. The foot of his crossed leg begins to beat a rhythm in the air, but he catches himself and stops it. Unlike his father, he works out. He has a large chest and shoulders, but he ignores his legs. She tries again.

"Did you know, he did not like the car?"

"What, wrong colour?"

"No. But, maybe he did not leave it to you because he did not like it."

"Right."

But he looks half-taken by this thought.

"Do you know why he did not like it? He bought it, remember, when he was made partner?"

Cameron looks at her.

"A vintage car, rare car, perfect in all ways. He did not like it, because he was supposed to love it."

Cameron snorts. "Sounds like him."

He stares off with a near-smile and she waits for whatever memory he is having to blossom and fade. She does not tell him about her own dislike of the car, following the time they were flying along the highway, top down, and as they approached and then flew past the concrete wall of an overpass he pretended to suddenly turn into it, to kill them instantly. Ten seconds passed before he yelled over the sound of the wind, "*Ooops.*" She was furious. She was scared.

"So, you will have the car?"

"I'll think about it." Cameron's eyes have rimmed silver, and she can hear his father's background rhythmic murmur, like a mindless lullaby, a body killing itself with its own weight.

English judge, English judge.

Cameron shakes his head at his private thoughts. He is an uncomplicated boy, not a beast like his father.

"Do you that think he wanted to live?" she asks him.

She hears Bill's flesh and bones hitting the tub as she meets the sincere gaze of this son, and she sees Bill alive in the eyes. Nothing else of Cameron looks like Bill, but the eyes make all of him beautiful. He does not appear surprised by her question. His eyes are tearing all the more. She sees that, like her, he feels responsible. And he seems to know what she is asking. Exactly what she is asking.

"I don't know," he says.

"Why did he not love us enough to stay?"

He doesn't hesitate in saying, more softly, "I don't know."

"Me too," Chantal agrees. She is crying, but already eased by what he has said. This will help, to have a comrade. She thinks she can hear this.

Petterick

Peter gazed at nothing and the uncle watched the football game—so why did it feel like they were staring hard over their glasses at each other? Today as on all Sundays it was torture to wait here with him, Lily's Uncle Ray, the way he sat with both arms splayed along the couch back like a lounging Jesus, how some fingers nervously tapped while a knee jigged—a portrait of a martyr doing his duty and straining at the ropes. At the nails!

Peter snorted wisely.

"What?" The wiry uncle turned to him, smiling.

"Nothing. A kind of pun."

Uncle Ray watched him until he saw no more was coming, then looked back to the game.

"So, less than nothing," Peter added.

At this, her uncle blinked once, hard and long.

Just as unbearable was the smell here. It was a kind of breath gone deeply off, meat-sickness at its base, and today as always he imagined someone's floating intestinal bacteria, unhinged and potent in his nose—Peter had to stop this train of thought that made him breathe shallow, that kept him on the edge of his seat. But whose breath? Lily, almost thigh to thigh with him on buses after movies, offered up ordinary breath with its evidence of popcorn or garlic or movie-nap. So he'd checked her mother and her uncle—nothing—and yet their apartment festered on. Maybe under the sink a rat had slipped behind things while signing off, its pace of rot stealthily mild.

Whatever the smell's source, Lily would soon emerge through it from the dark hallway like a contradiction. She wouldn't fit because she was beautiful. Peter was almost certain she was beautiful.

But as usual Lily was taking her time emerging, and here in the living room Uncle Ray kept him company with limp chat and questions, stuff you could answer with your tongue alone. (From some shadowed distance Peter heard a drawer softly thunk. What delicious thing was Lily doing?)

Though Ray had angled to engage in conversation, he couldn't not glance at the football scramble on the screen and now his glance had grown permanent. The man wore a constant near-smirk; he seemed always about to say, with avuncular irony, "Here I am doing my duty, and there you are perched on the edge of your seat, a nervous suitor." But someone like Ray would never say something like that. The smirk was camouflage, just like—again Peter snorted wise—his own shallow breathing and perching wasn't what it seemed.

Tired of pretending to care about the quarterback who'd unretired and come back to resurrect the Jets, Peter decided to speak. Why he used the English accent he wasn't sure, because usually he reserved it for those brief, singsong arguments he tended to have with café waiters: Looking up from the menu, "Is it really?" Looking into one's cup, "Are you sure?"

He said this: "You don't suppose it's somehow telling that we're all, um, practitioners of the non-nuclear family?"

Accent or not, there followed a gap, into which Uncle Ray leaned and squinted, as if his hearing were the problem. He uncrossed his legs. He said, "I'm not sure exactly what ..."

Peter meant that Lily, at thirty, shared an apartment with a mother and an uncle. He told Ray that this resembled the leavings of a large family culled by war. He added, "Maybe you didn't know I live alone?"

"Well, hey, no. I didn't." Uncle Ray still looked less than comprehending as he regarded Peter warily. The screen-scramble began again and Peter was happy to make him miss a play. He was also happy that Lily had escaped the genes of that long nose.

Peter helped. "Alone. You can't be less nuclear than that, I don't think."

"I guess not."

"In that a nucleus needs—" Peter raised his eyebrows encouragingly.

"Stuff around it, sure."

Peter could see that this conversation had caused Ray to like him even less. In fact Ray looked desperate. Perhaps he'd just leave for once, which would be excellent. Peter wasn't sure if the mother was home. Imagine if he and Lily had the place to themselves! He would walk in that direction, at last. Her bed. He'd seen it once, the first time he'd come, thirteen weeks ago, when Lily and her non-nuclear family had given him the tour.

Through the musk of his wish Peter saw Ray's spasm, heard the whispered "Always on Sunday." Peter didn't care. The man was perfectly named. Ray was thin, tanned, focused, a beam of American hotdog.

At least Ray hadn't asked the usual "How's school?" Its scorn so subtle it was all the more barbed. How could it not be scorn? Peter was in Linguistics; why would Ray call it *school*? An elementary word that carried the question, Why is someone your age still in it? And, sure, perhaps Ray had a case, Lily no doubt having described Peter's flight from English to Art History, back to English—this time Olde and with a Latin buttress—then to Biology, and now Linguistics, a search spanning over a decade. He would get a degree in another year if … but in any case, honest indecision was no cause for scorn. Unlike *decision*, which led countless men like Uncle Ray to lives of quiet desperation in retail.

A faint snap of plastic on plastic had both men turn their faces to it. The female noise had travelled far, down corridors, through closed doors. Peter found it such an of-a-sort apartment. Probably luxurious back when, expensive in any case, the three-bedroom felt if anything too spacious, all in that yellow-beige whose fade suggests dirt despite being clean. Its sprawl of walls needed tightening, and more pictures wouldn't do it. Though two storeys up a reasonable brownstone, it reminded Peter, impossibly, of the word *rancher*. The only thing missing was a wet bar fronted by thick grout bearing multicoloured riverstones.

Or maybe it was just that Lily was off down that dim hall and too far away.

Uncle Ray's body still angled at him for conversation but his head pointed directly away at football and was holding there, a man twisted in duty. A shoulder was also up as a kind of barrier. One team was yellow and black while the other was a dark cat-grey that flashed to mallard. Up ahead lay Super Bowl Sunday, when one of these teams would be alive and the other golfing, said the commentator.

LILY HAD ONCE CALLED HIM "a throwback," careful to laugh and squeeze his biceps when she said it. Peter loved her for that. In his sparse social life, he felt he was little more than a repository for signals, most of them bad: he was old-fashioned, awkward, he was some arrogant curio. Rarely were the signals ... affectionate squeezes.

Once, on the bus, after his knowing quip about Nicole Kidman's height, wherein he used the terms "emasculation" and "kindly camera angle," she called him "suave." She said it with cheerful amazement, as if identifying a force no longer in vogue. Peter smiled simply and lifted an eyebrow for her.

And the best signal of all came in the café near the movie theatre. Her latte done, she'd interrupted him as he pressed biscotti crumbs from his plate while wondering aloud about Chomsky and how the word "cranky," meaning whiny, likely had its origins in "crank," meaning genius-nobody-listened-to, or maybe it was the other way around, but wasn't it telling that linguistics could lead to concerns of global— She grabbed both his hands in hers, found his eyes and wouldn't let them go as she said, "You are *so* decent-looking for a duck." She had called him an "odd duck" enough times to trim it down for humour, and for intimacy.

Decent-looking. Holding his hands. The main difference between Lily and every other girl he'd ever spoken to was that most of her signals were good.

"SO YOU TWO OFF to your movie?" Uncle Ray didn't meet his eye in the asking, but he seemed to have healed because his near-smirk was back.

"We're—not sure." It felt almost risqué, saying this. Yes, it was Sunday and Sundays they went to a movie, but no, they weren't *sure*. Ray? If you're talking about Lily and Peter, anything might happen.

Ray stood quickly, as if he hadn't believed Peter's boast of not being sure and was going to have it out with him right now.

"Well, I'm off. To do some things. You can just"—Ray flicked a finger at the kitchen, then the remote control, and then, sadly it seemed, at the TV—"make yourself at *you* know."

Peter stood to shake the uncle's hand. "Okay, Ray," he said, pumping a surprisingly obedient limb twice, then letting it go. Ray glanced back once more at the game.

It was more or less always this way. Though their time together was civilized, they mutually dismissed each other with signals that were clear.

"LILY AND PETER" was better than "Peter and Lily." He explained to her that "Lily and Peter" began and ended with soft vowels and rose like a mountain on the two hard *e*'s of the middle. "Peter and Lily" was just a bumpy rural road. Lily confessed to not liking her name. Peter asked if this was because her tongue bumped her palette twice so quickly. She said she didn't know; maybe it was that she couldn't live up to a flower, flowers being perfect and never smelling bad—she shot him a look and he wondered if she was acknowledging her apartment. Her father's nickname for her had been Tiger-Lily, then just Tiger. She told Peter he died when she was eight, and Peter could see in her eyes the memories that were now burnished false. In any case, he then snorted at his own name, which he announced he detested. Why? asked Lily. Because, he answered, he was an idiot Principle. He was robbed to pay Paul, and he was mocked for being a Pumpkin Eater. Also, he didn't have a longer, more elegant name for sanctuary, like Richard could help a Rick, or Robert saved a Bob. Even as a child he'd wished he had a Petterand or Petterick to ascend to, like rising into a regal posture that was his birthright.

Lily smiled here and looked over her glasses to say, "Hello, Petterick."

Yes, and worst—he'd continued, but only in his mind—like all Peters everywhere he had to deal with the life absurdity of a given name that had also been given to the penis. Imagine: whenever a male suitor named Peter came to sit and wait and stare down a dark hallway and picture her beside that tautly made bed, smoothing on a cream, eyeing the flirt of a curl, spraying something lovely onto something lovelier, how could she hear his name and not see a *peter* perched too alertly on the edge of the couch, panting like a coyote?

RAY LEFT IN A FLURRY of keys, elbows, sleeves, and finally door, then there was a silence so complete it couldn't contain a mother; it simply couldn't.

Peter didn't know what to do. He'd already flicked off the TV as a kind of rebuke when Ray had turned in search of shoes, and it would be a defeat to flick it back on. The magazines he could see through the coffee-table glass were identical to those he disdained while waiting to have a molar steadied or testicle checked. He was too wound up to read anyway. If he looked inside himself, he saw all nerves roaring. If he looked deeper, he could see that this nervousness was but a small part of something far bigger; nervousness was just the face, or maybe even the hair, of a monstrous hunger. And he was tired of it. This long string of Sundays was about one thing: the hope of one day being invited to her bed. Others used dancing or walks or dinners, pick your ritual. Theirs had been Sunday movies, most of them in and of themselves meaningless, cinematic rehashes of the blindingly familiar, as if only childish verbs were used in the storyline, so that in the aftermath bus ride, no adult words were worth wasting on them. But if this string of Sundays hadn't been a long bus route to sex, what had it been? If Darwin was even half right, every breath he'd ever taken was sexy respiration meant to keep him alive for—this afternoon.

The smell had somehow grown worse. He peered through it down her hallway. She had so much power, and he had none. He was more than tired of this. He stood.

Because wasn't this the ultimate signal? The kind that knowing girls sent to awkward boys all over the globe? A boy perched and ready, a girl ear-cocked and waiting. Would any leading man in any movie not heed this signal? Not stand and go to her? Even Forrest Gump would have read this one. Woody Allen would have gone three times by now.

Maybe she saw it differently. Maybe she thought she had no power. Waiting for him in her room, maybe she saw the power to be all his, this power of advance, which did indeed seem to belong to the man. A power to *take her yet again*. Good God.

Peter found himself padding softly, entering the hallway's shadow. His plan was to knock on the mother's door when he came to it, and if she appeared he would claim a search for the bathroom—a known door he had already passed, but no matter, since she was the kind of matron whose smile grew when correcting stupid boys. And now he stood at the mother's door. The smell grew more vile here, but he didn't want to consider this. He rapped a single knuckle on the wood, deftly casual. His body had steeled itself for mother-rage, an explosion that would blow off his clothes then attack him for the nakedness.

No one. No uncle, no mother. Standing in the way, no one but himself.

Confidence, Peter said to his legs, getting them to move again, *is charming*.

He manoeuvred the hallway, trying not to wonder about that bed, or how this might go. He stopped at and pretended to be interested in a painting, in folk-art mode, of a red boat and white dock and two coils of very yellow rope. He pretended to care that such a bright painting had been relegated to shadow. Then, taking three side steps, he stopped, for here was her door—which was also in a frame, a coffin-shaped trap set for hall-walking men. Maybe she would guide him. He knew that for all their show of innocence, women were connected to earth in the deep ways. They were the bowl and the man but the spoon. Or the spigot. Maybe the bent faucet. One of Peter's knees buckled. Maybe, maybe she would help him. If he was confident enough to let her.

The smell had grown again. Peter lost his mind and knocked.

"Yes?" It was a sound of surprise. But they are actors.

"I've come … to see your room again."

Lily opened her door just as he finished speaking and said, "Oh," giving away nothing. Light streamed from behind her, darkening her hair and making her head look smaller. But what he could see of her face was beautiful. She added, "Aren't you worried about the movie?" They toss out diversionary signals in counterpoint to the main one.

"No."

"I was hurrying but I couldn't get off the phone. We were having a bit of— Okay, come on in, I guess."

Peter had not exactly pushed past her but he'd entered confidently, a blood-pounding feeling of incandescence. He stood in the room's centre, surveying it, hands on hips, incandescence fading. He nodded once, but that felt foolish. He didn't look at the bed.

Now Lily was acting at nervousness. "But you really like this director. What's his—?"

Because he was in socks he felt too short. Though she was in socks too. The smell was even worse in here.

"Who were you talking with?"

"I've been wanting to tell you about Michael, but—"

"*Everybody* has a Michael."

"Sorry?"

"Everybody has a *Michael.* Every *Mike* has a Michael to—"

"Peter? This one is what you'd call a boyfriend. Maybe. I'm not sure. But, Peter? You never seemed to show much interest in, I don't know, 'me,' so Michael was a kind of— What are you … ?"

He was lying on her bed, not sure how he'd got there or what he was doing. A sob almost came out, but it would have been fake. A moan sounded right, one suggesting he was on this bed against his will. Then an "um" in the English accent. Then a short, soft whistle. Nothing he did could be trusted.

"Peter?"

He was on the bed. He'd landed. It was a kind of big bang, because here he was void of thought, at the still point, at ground zero, with his atoms flying away in all directions. He coughed, and then he was sort of laughing, and in a wobbly voice it all came out of him, as he jerked with laughter, then a sob that was possibly not fake. He couldn't tell how she took any of it: the apology, the declaration of love, his hunt for sex today, *I had designs on you* confessed while shaking his head, him an absurd virgin at twenty-nine, an awkward idiot, he probably had a syndrome, unique and undiagnosable, he had *Petterick*, he was frozen and doltish at what everyone else on earth could do well and easily. At some point during this outburst he'd flipped to nose into her pillow, smelling it deeply. It smelled wonderful, almost a talc. And now Lily was on the bed too.

She sat beside him, fingers on his neck. She told him not to get her pillow wet, but she said it affectionately and with humour, a signal that she at least considered him the kind of buddy who'd also see the humour.

"I don't know what to do," she said.

"Frame it," he said, tapping the pillowcase, being that buddy. She had several times joked that his used napkin or ticket stub should be framed because he would be famous someday, though for what she never said. He had never written a poem, never tweaked software.

"No," she said. "It's— Well, Peter? I thought you were gay. Or, you know, I 'wondered.' The movies, always on Sunday. You never, ever—"

"So Sunday's the gay day?"

"No, but *you* know."

After a pause, just long enough to deepen her voice, Lily added, "The thing is, I've always found you, actually, very good-looking." The fingers on his neck grew warmer, more silken, their multi-digit signal somehow hinting at rhythm. Then the fingers were removed.

The sudden removal was bad. It felt possibly terminal. Though her hip was an inch from his, though they were on a bed, this gap was— He needed to decide something, say something and say it now. And what he said had to be—

But it was Lily who spoke.

"So let's take a shower."

Her fingers landed back on his neck. Playful now. Sporting.

"A shower?"

"That thing where water sprays magically out of the wall?"

"Now?"

She nodded.

"At the same time?" he said.

"It is written. Nobody's here."

Lily led him up by the hand. She jerked him comically across the dark hallway when he hesitated. Not knowing what to say he said nothing as clothes fell around their feet and Lily reached in to turn on taps. They stood quietly naked for a weird span of time before she sent a hand in to test the temperature. Weirder, neither of them dropped their eyes below chin level. Peter aimed blindly and placed his hand on her naked hip, and Lily let him. He was about to step in for their first hug, which would be naked, but she led him into the spray.

And then they were hugging, they were hugging and moving, and she brought soap into the mix, and he was quickly almost delirious. There, a squat white tile bench was built into the wall, and upon it glorious things were going to happen.

Her angel's mouth was breathing an inch from his ear.

"Peter, I've also wanted to tell you that you really—you really—need to shower more often. I've been meaning to say something."

"I smell?" He pulled his cheek away from hers. "That's—" He was unable to look at her. "That's been me?" His hold on her shoulders softened. The glorious warm spray had become mere water. It was a world going limp.

Lily pulled back to reassure him at arm's length. She smiled so beautifully that Peter could only believe all she said.

"Look, here we are. Lovers have to be honest. Don't we?" She stared at him, naked and smiling, and he was an empty baby. "Isn't this okay?"

"Yes."

"It's nothing. It's a small thing."

"It's fine."

"There's always soap!"

"There's ... never not soap."

"It's even funny. Uncle Ray," she said, skewing her mouth to signal a joke and shaking her head fondly, "he called it 'a deal killer.' Well, look how wrong he was." She did so, taking in the proof of the shower, the walls, even the ceiling, and then their feet.

"Uncle Ray." Peter shook his head as if fondly too. "He's a unique *kind*," he said, boldly letting the oxymoron stand.

They came together and kissed, Petterick's first. And as he rose again to delirium, apparently Darwin's main signal of success, he noted the knowing dance of their lips and tongues, a wet and glorious language that was very much beyond him.

Geriatric
Arena
Grope

When Vera Barnoff got home and in the door her phone stopped ringing, then almost immediately started again, so she knew it must be something important. Her heart flipped in the foolish hope it was the doctor's office with glorious news that they'd mixed up the lab work and she was fine. But it turned out to be good news anyway—she picked up to learn her daughter, Lise, had scored three tickets for tomorrow night.

Lise snorted when Vera used the word "scored"—sixty-seven-year-old mothers didn't use such words. Except they did.

"Well, happy birthday, Mom." Lise paused. "So I'll phone Dad?"

"It'd be wasted on him."

"He said he'd go."

"That's different than wanting to go. Most people'd kill to go."

Lise was silent, wouldn't give up on her father.

"Or, Lise? We'll scalp it!"

"Yes!" Lise wasn't serious, but into the spirit.

"For booze and drug money!"

She'd deflated her daughter again—mothers didn't talk about booze and drugs. Vera could've added that Leonard

Cohen himself was older than she was, had tried every drug known to man and chose a Scotch-guzzler for a guru. Her daughter had somehow missed the wisdom that it's okay to play, it really is. Though maybe she wasn't as stiff with her friends. But God, she wasn't even forty.

"Thanks for doing all that work, dear." She knew Lise had had to bypass Ticketmaster, among other nefarious and complicated things. She'd probably spent lots of money.

"Mom, no, I love this too! Did you read the review?"

"Which one, dear?" Vera had been reading them all. He was roaming the continent. Leonard was coming to town.

"I don't know but it said he *skips* off the stage, between sets."

"It'll be fun."

"The first note of 'Hallelujah' I'm going to be crying."

"It'll be fun," Vera said again. It would be. Lise's enthusiasm sounded real, and for decades Vera had never not been buoyed by the sound of her child's excitement. She believed it was in the tone of voice itself and was neurological. An electric signal to a mother's brain, pulsing, *All is for the moment right.* Life was simple sometimes. For the moment, she could feel in perfect health.

LISE'S GAMBITS TO GET Vera and Mac back together were touching. She'd been at it ever since learning they were meeting again for lunches and even a few dinners. Dates, Lise liked to call them. Once Vera had told her that she and her father had "hooked up" the night before and Lise did a comic shudder, but it might have been real.

Lise understood what had happened nine years ago because they told her everything. Mac had had an affair with a rather young substitute teacher at the high school where both he and Vera taught—Mac English, Vera biology. Vera told Lise that though her father's affair coincided with his forced retirement at sixty-five, a psychologically difficult time for him, it was no excuse. Vera stayed on at the school, where everybody knew, and it had meant "the death of my pride." She explained further that it was animal pride, the kind that does not heal.

So Lise understood why they'd separated nine years ago, but during that entire time she'd been eager for the merest hint of reconciliation. Not long after they sold the house and bought their separate condos, Lise informed Vera that according to her pedometer, she and Mac lived barely eight hundred steps from each other. Lise shared this fact with a wry smile, the same smile she would probably use to say, "You still love each other. Quit pretending." This year Lise had one of her own two children graduating from the high school Vera and Mac had both retired from, but she still acted the hopeful child of a broken home.

Lise, darling Lise. Vera remembered how Mac let her name their child Lise, Vera's desire being to grab something French Canadian. Something of Montreal. She still thought it her hometown, could still conjure the smell of any given season, as well as certain alleys.

MAC CALLED HER that night pretending to be mad. "How do you know I wouldn't kill to go?" he said.

So it was clear how much detail Lise had betrayed. Just as she told Vera that Mac had asked her why someone her age would go see Leonard Cohen if she wasn't being paid to. Mac was always being funny. Or, at least, was always not serious. It was hard to know what to call his constant light mockery of everything, including himself. Last week he'd told Vera his autobiography would be called *Canoeing in Azkaban: My Fictiony Life*. Only later did Vera get that it referenced not the Middle East but Harry Potter.

"You don't like Leonard Cohen," Vera said into the receiver.

"Actually I do."

"You've told me you don't. I have his music and I remember—I remember clearly—you yanking it off at a party."

"He's not party music. I'd yank 'The Volga Boatmen' off too."

"He's uplifting."

"So's a choir. A choir can't party either."

Mac had her smiling a little. For some reason, this firmed up her decision not to tell him the news. It could wait. Mostly, she didn't want Lise to know, not yet. And it still might be nothing. The doctor called them shadows.

"Anyway, I do want to come. I need to protect my women from the Great Seducer."

"It's up to Lise. She got the tickets."

"The only Canadian in history who tries to fuck everything in sight."

"Stop."

"I won't go if you don't want me to go."

"Fine. Go. Come."

"You know I saw your big droning Leonard way back when?"

"No, you didn't."

"Well yes, I did. Amsterdam or—"

"You would have told me this."

"I probably did tell you. Probably a hundred years ago."

"Really?" She recalled having arguments about Leonard in the past, and you'd think that during one he'd have mentioned seeing him live, if only to use as leverage, as he was doing now. Or was it possible that this was an old man's long-term memory kicking in, as they said it would? The old bag tipping over, spilling the long-lost shiny bits? The childhood hamsters and bicycles?

"It was Amsterdam, I think. It was outside. There were screamers and the sound was horrible. That's all I remember. But, Vera? Screamers? For a poet? And shitty sound, when the only important thing is the words?"

Words were not the only important thing. She was more convinced now that Mac didn't appreciate Leonard.

"Anyway, may I come?"

"You may."

"But now you have to ask me nicely."

They hung up eventually and Vera wasn't angry with him. He well knew that Leonard was her unassailable all-time favourite, and that to insult him was to mock her. She saw where it came from: Mac was biologically compelled to attack Leonard because both men were seventy-four. Mac didn't see a beautiful man, poet, singer, sufferer. He saw a rival. This didn't make her think less of him. Boys would be boys. Vera supposed she was glad her ex still had some juice.

SHE KNEW SHE WOULDN'T SLEEP, and she didn't. She moved from bed to recliner and back, and the night passed not too horribly. Other tests were pending. She could hear the calm voice of the young oncologist, who had even risked a joke. After describing for the second time a long list of possible options and outcomes, he paused, hefted her ever-thickening file, eyed it wickedly and said, "Or maybe we can bore it to death."

The worst came around 3 a.m. Sitting in her chair watching figure skating, she suffered a bout of self-pity possibly triggered by the girls' youth and bodies, and she cried for minutes. When she emerged, she had a clear understanding that she would tell no one anything until her news was certain.

Between trips into her bedroom to tempt unconsciousness, she distracted herself with cups of chamomile and her "meditation walk," where she held a small crystal ball in cupped hands at belt level and walked slowly but aimlessly, with a purposefully open mind, trying to be a big version of the crystal. Despite these measures, not only fear but memories swelled. About Mac, and about his affair. For this she blamed the Leonard disc she'd put on, as songs of love naturally kindled thoughts of it. Mac, she loved. And hated. It still felt that simple. Her name was Trisha. Vera had met her. She was no beauty, beyond the kind automatically bestowed by two fewer decades of life lived. It had lasted just three months. But sex *was* love. Leonard knew

this. Not many men did. Which made it tragic, which made
it a poem. Mac didn't know, he'd called it a lark, he'd called it
a desperate flight from age. But it had been love, because he'd
wanted it to be love. Men always wanted it to be love, even if
they wouldn't admit it to themselves.

Vera took the music off on her way to heat some milk,
thinking about Mac mocking such poetry. Maybe the retired
English teacher could be forgiven his arrogance. Mac had read
so much and gave such thought to what he read so he could
share those thoughts with his students. Under the surface glaze
of irony, for over forty years he'd tried hard, nobly hard. All his
efforts to slide what he called "the good stuff," the iconoclasts—
his beloved Beats, mostly—under the radar of the latest school
board. He cared. She could so easily picture him standing tall up
there at the front, gazing over their faces, cracking wise, having
a worthy time. She was saddened by Mac's bitterness when he
joked, "I taught maybe two percent of the kids I taught." She'd
countered that he'd helped many more to consider the weight
of words. To which he said, "Okay, sure. Three."

Vera stood, cupping her warm milk. She blew ripples onto
its steaming surface, blowing a crust to the edge, where it rose
and buckled, a thinnest bone. Because he thought too much,
Mac couldn't hear Leonard's words. They were fire that melted
contradictions. His voice the crucible. He was an alchemist,
turning pain into beauty. Leonard used his own pain, you could
tell. Mac didn't see the stick-thin boy, a human antenna who
walked Montreal when it still hid pockets of the old country,
a last bastion of fat mothers with flour down the vast slope of
their chests, of men-only taverns for cigar-smokers with hats

and huge egos. A Jewish boy from a Catholic city, living his mature years under a Zen priest. Who loved to guzzle Scotch! Contradictions. The biggest one, that of men and women, a gulf he'd learned to cross with ease. Perhaps he was so wise a man because he was half woman. He would be lazy and selfish in bed, but hearing one word from you his eyes would clear, and deepen, and they would become a mirror. He would know the clitoris and where it rooted in your brain. And then he turned you into a song.

In her living room chair, she found herself sadly smiling. If she had the guts to say any of this to Mac, if he wasn't angered into silence he'd scoff up a storm. How could she tell him that, if Leonard seduced you, you could only be eager, because in sleeping with Leonard you were also, for the first time, sleeping with yourself? And that listening to him sing would be as close as she would ever get to that?

She padded to the kitchen to eat a banana, staring out the window with its decent view of the southern foot of Victoria, the strait, the Olympic Mountains beyond. At night, the city lights simply stopped at the pure blackness that meant water. That ancient night—how utterly lonely, and how much more powerful than the fragile lights, each of which could be killed with the flick of a finger. Or all of them with one storm. This city, all cities, would one day rejoin that powerful black. Full of spirit, or just black? What would Buddhist Leonard say to that one?

Finding an odd inscrutable comfort, she continued gazing out over the imagined water. Lately there'd been local resistance to the name change, from the Strait of Georgia to the Salish

Sea. Victoria was so fucking British. Mac's own mother—startlingly flat-chested, posture of a flagpole—would have been angry to know they were going to see a Jewish singer, one who had enjoyed a string of women. Vera could see her snort of disgust.

NEXT AFTERNOON, SHE jigged balsamic into the tabbouleh, laid a sprig of mint on top, snapped a lid on the bowl and slid it into the fridge to chill. Predictably, Vera's sleeplessness now felt like she rode an iffy raft down an unknown river. Lots of energy but it all might topple and sink. Soon Lise would arrive with her father, whom she'd pick up on her way and drive him those eight hundred steps. Vera had decided not to tell them their dinner was Leonard-themed. It was silly guesswork anyway. The man's favourite nosh might be pork roast for all she knew, or more likely he'd gone vegan, propped up with coffee and Scotch. She just based it on where he'd lived. The bagel chips and cream cheese and kosher dill appetizer plate was obvious. But then the tabbouleh and grilled lamb loin with lime juice and coarse salt. Some Ben & Jerry's pistachio for dessert, and Turkish coffee. Good California merlot throughout, though Mac was down to a single glass at a time and Lise was driving.

The evening began well, despite a new and suspicious ache between her shoulder blades, one that seemed to grab when she swallowed. Hard to ignore, but the bustle of hosting helped. As did *Greatest Hits*, both 1 and 2. Lise presented her with the three tickets wrapped in red ribbon with an oversized bow. Sitting gangly and stooped in her best chair, like he always did, though maybe of late looking more vulture-like, Mac kept his sarcasm to a minimum. He asked in apparent seriousness if it was wise to listen to Cohen's well-produced studio work just hours before "hearing him old and live and rough" in the bad acoustics of the Memorial Centre. Lise, sometimes very much her father's daughter, said, "You're old and live and rough, and you sound okay."

Then, just when the timer buzzed to tell her the lamb needed to go under the broiler, Vera caught Mac smiling at her, mockery in his eyes. He held a dill in one hand and a bagel chip in the other, and he waggled both. He knew her that well.

She left for the kitchen without reaction. Basically, there was something she needed to know about Mac: How much was he on her side, really? How much had he ever been on her side?

She shook her head, almost a spasm, and concentrated on dinner, on tonight, her rushing raft making it almost hard to see. The lamb had bleached pale from the lime and looked so tender and superb it beckoned any good bohemian carnivore to eat it raw. With his lips—Vera mused—he will take it raw from your palm, in the dim hallway, under a crucifix, on your way to the bedroom.

She reset the timer and returned to the living room. It was like he'd been on his best behaviour until now. Maybe it was the two glasses of wine, Mac kicking out the stops before a rock concert.

"Did you hear," he asked of the sunset-lit window between Vera and Lise, "how he got ripped off by his manager, lost his whole pile, and this tour is a scramble to get some cash back? And resume the lifestyle to which he is tra-la-la?"

"I thought he was a Buddhist," said Lise. "Living simply and all that." Then she nodded for her father. "But I do remember reading something like that. Big embezzlement thing."

"He's quit the Buddhism," Mac added. "Came down off that particular mountain."

"No, he hasn't," Vera put in, too loudly. She settled back into the couch and cleared her throat before continuing. "Did you read what he said about religion in general? He was asked about his years on Mt. Baldy, his retreat there, and he said it's all the same, religions are all the same, and that everyone should follow the religion of their ancestry. Their culture."

"Their childhood," offered Lise, her eyes oddly bright. She'd never gone to church of any kind.

"Exactly," said Vera.

"That," said Mac, actually pointing a finger at her, "is such a Zen thing to say. Go ask every Zen master on the block if you should study Zen, every one'll say, 'No!' Actually, they'd say, '*God* no!'"

Vera eventually got them seated. They ate, her cooking was praised, and she managed to keep the subject on other things.

Then Mac shot Vera the briefest glance before announcing to Lise, "You know, I saw Lenny way back when."

"Did you!" Lise looked genuinely excited by this.

Lenny. Belittling a great man through his name. He sometimes called Obama "The Story of O."

"Actually, maybe twice. Once in Europe, for sure. Amsterdam." He paused, looking at Lise. "I was paid to go."

He didn't smile saying this, but his deadpan was like one big wink.

"Dad, we're not making you go."

"No, I'm comin', I'm comin'," he chirped.

"Good"—Lise consulted her watch—"because we're leaving in ten minutes. Gulp your wine. Finish your ice cream."

Vera dutifully scraped up the several pistachios she'd left to soak in the melted ice cream in the bottom of her bowl.

"It'll be this," Mac announced. "The lights go down and he goes all deep and croony and these emotions big as big wet sponges all over us paid-to-go guys, it'll be this huge grope fest. For old girls. Lenny's geriatric arena grope."

From the way he lurched forward to grab another bagel chip, Vera saw how proud he was of that one.

"I don't want you to come." Vera didn't look at him. She didn't want him even that close to her. "I mean it. I'm serious." She closed her eyes, nodded.

When Lise saw that Vera wasn't retracting, she said, "C'mon, Mom."

Mac was predictably silent. One eyebrow up, he stared through the table.

"You try to fuck everything in sight." She added, more quietly, "And you can't quite do it."

"Jesus, Mom," Lise whispered, shaking her head almost invisibly.

"I'm serious, Mac. You'll ruin it for me." She glared at him and he met her eye. *Lenny's geriatric arena grope*—he'd already ruined it. She would carry this with her into the concert and it would colour the whole event. His words still worked too well on her. She needed to be free of him. She should move from this city.

Mac gazed at the floor now, his eyebrow back up.

To Lise she said simply, "We're dropping him off."

MAC DIDN'T BEG, and they drove a severely quiet eight hundred steps back to his building. On the way downtown Lise spoke only when spoken to, angry but hiding it, pretending that driving took a certain concentration. Vera knew her daughter wouldn't befoul tickets she'd spent so much on, nor would she ruin a birthday. In the silence (they'd decided against playing Leonard in the car) Vera considered revealing her news, which would mean instant forgiveness, but she didn't like her new motivation, so she resisted. And Vera figured she already sucked her daughter like a vampire. In any case, she wanted to keep it inside awhile longer. To release it would feel like contagion, in the car, into the night. Held inside, it stayed smaller.

They parked with difficulty and it was almost late, so they had to hurry. Vera still rode the rushing river of no sleep and her raft was tipping. She could hardly wait for that voice. She hoped it didn't put her to sleep, his voice also being the warmest bath; it would be embarrassing, and a shame to miss a minute. She had the badly startling notion that her new swallowing ache wouldn't let her sleep, not in the concert and not later.

They approached the arena in a mist blown into their faces by a wind growing nastier. Downtown smelled like downtown, of exhaust and faint piss, like old Montreal, like the haunch of poetry, Victoria did have some charm. Vera clutched the three tickets in her coat pocket, still bound by the crimson ribbon and bow. The arena's wide-open doors accepted mostly hustling stragglers now.

Vera heard the man's voice just as she reached the door, a forlorn voice, almost a mumble, about tickets, did anyone maybe have a ticket to sell? She didn't hesitate, but ripped one from the ribbon and marched it over to him. He was unshaven, skinny, maybe thirty, an impoverished grad-student look. Fairly handsome behind the bulky glasses, which he seemed to wear as a foil to his good looks. She turned away saying, "A gift," and she was already at the door when he called his thanks.

They hurried to find their tunnel, Vera warbling to herself, "Oooo, this'll be great," and "I can hardly wait," Lise dutifully agreeing. They climbed to their row. They side-stepped past knees then sat and flung off scarves and flapped their arms out of coats just as the lights fell to an instant surprising roar. In that last light she had noticed the empty seat to her left. Legs passed clumsily in front of her, bumping her knees—only now did she understand that of course the young man with her ticket would be sitting here right beside her.

Stage spots came up, and there was his band and his girl backup singers. To another roar out came Leonard, wearing his fedora and looking decades out of place and wise for it. Here he was, somehow still elegant, a bit mantis-like but spry. His walk was disarming, it betrayed some shyness. He arrived at the mic and noise fell at this simple promise. Smiling, Leonard looked around to see all the loving faces, as though harsh light was no obstacle to this.

"Please," Vera said into Lise's ear as she took her daughter's hand, "just for one song." Vera turned to the young man at her left, got him to look at her and asked, smiling, horrified at herself, "Can I please hold your hand for just one song?" He smirked, but with a dog's distrust in his eyes as Vera took his hand out of his lap. And so she sat, holding two hands— one mechanical, the other fearful. She raised them both and stretched her arms out to either side of her, which opened her breastbone, and she imagined her whole life blooming out of her. She closed her eyes and felt all the shadows, so many of them, some turning at her to knuckle her heart or bite it tooth- lessly. She released a long, an endlessly long breath, felt herself relax in a way that might be hazardous. The singing started.

She bucked with instant crying, her smile wide open and sloppy. It felt strange not to bring her hands to her face. Tears fell cold and fresh down her cheeks. Poor Mac. Who only tried, his best, to be free. He should be here. He should be here.

The voice took her from the front. Black like blood, it entered on elegance, and brought heat. Kneeling at every cell of her body, her soles and her scalp, it asked its one question. She was a responsive lover. Over the music, she felt but couldn't hear herself wailing her answer.

To
Mexico

The first night, Dale was standing by himself on the balcony, in the early dark. Somehow he relaxed enough to notice the sky. "Relaxed" wasn't the word, it was more that he was worn down, not just by a day's airport grind but by the months at home that came before. On the balcony, gently mouth breathing, Dale was tiredly alert, and here was the moon, the famous curled white sliver, but instead of vertical it lay flat. Like a tiny coy smile. A tiny smile in a black face the size of eons. The size of the face and the size of the smile could hardly be comprehended together. He saw more: one pale star up in a far left corner of sky, and then up in the right corner, another. Two tiny eyes for the tiny smile. He had to pivot his head to see the whole face, which gave off wall-eyed irony the size of the universe. He tried to relax and feel amused by it. He knew a nose would appear if he looked for one.

He heard Anna emerge from the bathroom. When she clunked a glass down, loud on purpose, Dale turned from the comical sky to his worst nightmare, who wasn't looking at him from in there on the couch.

"Want some?" Anna waggled her empty glass in his direction.

"Sure," he said. "You should see this sky."

"It's completely dark out there."

"No, it's not," he said, regretting it right away, not wanting to show her the impossible face. She wouldn't get it. That is, she'd get it but wouldn't let herself enjoy it, the magical distortion, the brain stretch—because it was his idea. It had come to this. At one time she would have joined him and they'd have laughed together, excited by the size of space. She would have found the nose.

Anna brought Dale a tequila and sat in one of the balcony's wrought-iron chairs. She had refilled her glass; he'd see how that went. Back when they were planning this trip, she'd asked him, straight-faced, "You think I'll do a Lowry down there?" Though a binge could happen anywhere, her joke haunted him. Tequila was a favourite poison, and here it was almost free. Her hangovers were when they usually almost ended it.

The chairs were heavy and ornate and Anna was surprised how comfortable hers was. Normally he didn't care for heights, and they were perched way up a hill, their balcony hanging cliff-like over Puerto Vallarta's southern outskirts and the sea. Maybe because it was dark and he couldn't properly see the danger, it couldn't grab his gut. Or maybe he was too drained to be afraid. Of anything. Chances were—he mused as he touched tequila to his lips—if things got ugly between them tonight, if they started coming apart, he just wouldn't care.

"It's beautiful here," she said to the darkness. It sounded like a peace offering.

"I knew I'd love it," Dale agreed. He added stupidly, "I really want to see an iguana."

"Hey. To Mexico. We did it." She held out her glass and they clinked. She tossed her whole drink back, so he did too.

That night there were no eruptions and no plummets off the cliff. Anna was tired too and there on the balcony they barely managed some mumbling about tomorrow's plans. She wanted to check out silver shops, he wanted to hire one of those boats to go snorkelling. They both wanted to eat authentic Mexican, and she asked him, still friendly, if he was going to challenge himself with hot sauces. They had one more tequila each, then yawned and stared dumbly into the dark. When they went in and she was in the bathroom, he scanned the TV channels to see if there'd be any point ever watching it, and when he came to bed Anna was asleep, her back to him.

Which was fine, which was as usual. And it would make things easier. They were intending to split up here. Nothing had been discussed or announced, but Dale was almost sure that this was her plan.

HE HIRED A BOAT for not very much money, making the arrangements at the public dock with a tall and handsome man, Vasiliev. Why the man had a Russian name, Dale never did learn. He announced the deal to Anna somewhat proudly because it included all snorkelling gear, which she'd thought they might have to buy. Now, chugging off toward Los Arcos, a trip that at this speed would take an hour, he wasn't pleased to be crammed on board with another couple and their two kids. They didn't look pleased either. His assumption had been that fifty bucks got them their own boat, an assumption that seemed to be shared by the dad, a guy older than him, maybe pushing forty. The boat had one seat too few and the dad was standing. At one point Dale shrugged at him but he didn't shrug back. His kids, a boy and a girl, looked about ten, and his wife never stopped rifling through her day pack for treats, lotions, water. The motor roared too loud to talk over. Vasiliev, apparently just the fixer, was back on the dock. Their captain was a Mexican with an eternal smile, caricature of a Mexican moustache and not much English.

But it was a beautiful afternoon. Anna leaned on the boat's side, face into the breeze, which blew her hair back, a whipping bronze flag. She let her eyes close. She was into her own day pack for the mickey of tequila and discreet sips. Disappointed by the silver prices, which were double what she'd expected and meant she probably wouldn't be buying anything, Anna had been quiet most of the day. She was in that mood where something badly startling might emerge.

Dale watched the slow approach of Los Arcos—small islets that arched high from the water. The breeze was a relief. He caught the dad's eye again, stood and pantomimed him coming and taking Dale's seat, and the dad waved, smiled this time, shook his head. He was fine clinging to an iron post, hand to his brow like a pirate.

It was paradise, it truly was. The swelling blue sea, the friendly heat, a quaint old boat that smelled of rust and bait, taking them somewhere they'd never been. Arcing frigate birds, diving pelicans. Chased by something larger beneath, schools of small fish thrashed at the surface where they ran out of water. The view landward was of old Puerto Vallarta, its white masonry, palm trees, wild green hills up behind, and then the hills above Conchas Chinas, where their villa was. Dale couldn't quite see their place, or their balcony, but he knew there were green and yellow parakeets in those trees. And, apparently, iguanas. What could be better? At one point Anna caught the captain's eye and pointed languidly at something off the bow. The captain slowed, quizzical, then pointed himself and shouted, *"Turta! Turta!"* Dale finally saw it, a turtle's head, maybe thirty yards off, a sleek black fist sticking out of the water, then it was gone. Anna had already ceased looking at it. The boy never did get to see it, and when the engine roared them back to speed again, he was crying.

A few minutes later, when the little guy had calmed down, and after another pull from her bottle, Anna gestured Dale in close and said, "Next time we're here, let's pick door number 3."

That she was mocking this boat, and his arrangements, was clear. He always despaired when Anna became a wilfully hateful person, because it wasn't her, it really wasn't. And when he pulled back and looked at her, what also became clear was that she mostly mocked the notion of a "next time." She smiled dramatically and falsely, and her eyes, her beautiful deep-sky hateful eyes, dared him to join her and say something back and take things up a notch.

Now the captain was pointing and shouting, *"Manta, manta!"* They slowed and all of them saw the black fin— identical to a shark's, a big one—cut the surface. And then another fin, ten or twelve feet from the first, the manta ray's second wing tip. A plankton eater, harmless.

"Are there any sharks here?" he asked the captain.

The captain thrust his finger at the gliding wing tips. "No shark. Manta!"

Dale shrugged and pointed all around them. "Sharks? Any sharks? Ever?"

"No way sharks, no way!" he yelled, smiling non-stop, shaking his head, for far too long a time. Dale didn't believe him. He could imagine every captain in town agreeing not to see the sharks they saw every day, keep the tourists coming.

THE THIRD NIGHT, they were in J's Corruption, a bar they chose for the name alone. Puerto Vallarta had lots of colourful bar names and they figured it was the gay influence. Some buildings, they'd noted, had rainbow flags painted on an outside white wall. J's was nearly full but people sipped at their pink or green margaritas as an afterthought, many heads propped on a hand, elbows on the table. It looked like the end of a long hot day. Dale had learned that, like them, most tourists arrived on a Saturday and left on a Saturday, and so, city-wide, each new batch went through the same rhythms of party and recovery. Anna, for one, had a formidable hangover from the night before. During the cruise back from Los Arcos, her first mickey of the day empty, she'd leapt off the bow at full speed, shouting in Spanish. But tonight she didn't show it. Dale was used to this, how she climbed up through her pain to appear pretty much normal. Because there's no way she wasn't in pain. She masked it well, though she wasn't saying much or meeting his eye. Dale stared at the severe part down the middle of Anna's head, wondered if that dark freckle had always been there.

He recalled how they'd decided on Mexico three years ago, after a particularly tectonic fight, the one that resulted in them reaffirming never, ever to have a child they were sure to ruin, and then also agreeing never to buy a place together. They were lying in bed after making restorative love and she was being wryly humorous, but in the air hung the dire truth that before long, one of these bouts would end them. At some point she'd said, "Let's at least get to Mexico." She'd said it twice.

They both had involvements with it, with Mexico, and neither had ever been. Years ago she'd written her MA thesis on *Under the Volcano* and it was her all-time favourite book. That it was deemed inappropriate for her high school English class—owing not to content but to difficulty—depressed her. And, also years ago, Dale loved Castaneda, enchanted by the instructive maybe-not-quite-fiction, the magic that just might be true, and he'd read them all. And so they'd often agreed it was a shame that they'd never made it down, to see the world of their favourite books.

Now that they were finally here, Dale wondered if she remembered having said it. *Let's at least get to Mexico.* Of course she did. All the travel plans had been made, and the bags checked, the flights taken, the bed turned back and the turtle spotted—all with those words chiming in her ears. It was almost grotesque to think about. He eyed her as she took medicinal sips of her margarita. No. What was grotesque was that he couldn't ask her. That they wouldn't talk about these things, their difficulties, was a mark of how far apart they were. Funny, but it used to be the opposite—it was a mark of how close they were that they didn't have to speak. This had been clear right off the bat—when they started having sex, maybe even at the party where they met, Jonathan's, that birthday—that they saw each other inside out, right to the embarrassing bones, without having to cloud the view with words. It was a starkest intimacy, and they decided to call it love. Yet somewhere along the way—though *they never talked about it*—the involuntary nakedness began to feel more chilling than warm, and under her biting gaze he lacked enough hands to cover himself up.

J's huge dance floor was empty. The music tended to retro, new wave. It was probably ten-thirty. Anna commented on how dead things were, flicking a finger at the seated crowd, distractedly sipping. Dale joked that, like them, everybody was trying to digest several days of tortillas and tequila. When she said nothing, he asked if she wanted to try another place.

"All these heads are knobs," she said, "waiting to be flowers."

Because they were at tables and the tables were in rows, the heads did look like a pattern of knobs in the dim light.

"Flowers?"

"Why not." She still didn't bother looking at him.

"What kind of flowers?"

"Crazy come-*hump*-me flowers, *I* don't know."

"Maybe peonies, dripping pheromones," he said. He wasn't funny like her but he was trying to go along, add to it, join in. That's all he was doing. "You know peonies? Those big, bulbous lush—"

"I know what peonies are."

"That have to be opened by ants? They're like weird foreplay machines."

"I know the peony."

"Why," he asked her, brave, or maybe just really tired, "do you hate me right now? Right this second?"

Anna turned away, shaking her head. She didn't hate him, the sadness said. Her look was desolate. He wouldn't be getting any straight answers from her. Maybe there were no straight answers to give, but she wasn't even going to try. The day before, snorkelling at Los Arcos, after they'd anchored and gotten into the mismatched masks and flippers, she'd had him swim with her around to the other side of the first islet where, making sure they hadn't been followed, they found a ledge about four feet deep to stand on. She doffed her bottoms and got him going and got herself going and they managed a fast one, underwater, surrounded by yellow and blue fish and the horrendous squalling of birds roosting on the island ledge twenty feet above their heads. Pelicans, frigates, boobies almost shoulder to shoulder. The smell of bird shit was so ripe that Dale felt its sour acid in his nose and throat once he got to breathing hard. Her seduction was aggressive and more of a dare than anything else: since they were in slapdash Mexico they might as well fuck in public. He truly didn't like it that those two small kids were a few fin-kicks around a corner. And he was still thinking about sharks, and what he'd do if he saw a manta wing tip. But he managed her dare, glad when it was over. She said only "Okey-dokey," caught her breath, squeezed his biceps, got her bottoms back on and swam away from him. Sex was never a problem for them.

Unless you saw it as the thing that had kept them together too long.

Sitting in J's Destruction, saying *"banyo"* under her breath, Anna stood and walked from their table, snapping her fingers and popping her hips to a Bowie, one of the dancey ones. For two days she'd been surprising Dale with Spanish words like *banyo*. She somehow knew the difference, in Spanish, between mackerel and tuna when she ordered a skewer from a vendor. Without resorting to a word of English, she had haggled over a T-shirt. She knew how to get the good tequila and the darker beer. She told him that *diablo* wasn't the real hot sauce. Had she been studying? When he asked her this she regarded him with cool concern and said, "You don't pay attention, do you?" It was the kind of accusation he no longer pursued.

She didn't go to the *banyo* but made right for the dance floor. It was a bad sign, maybe the worst sign of all, when she danced solo to start off an evening. As if conspiring with her, some staff person in the dark recesses flicked a switch the instant she set foot on the dance floor and it lit up in glaring red and blue squares, popping off and on randomly, hideously. If colour were noise, it would have been deafening.

After gulping all the ice-mush of his margarita so fast he got brain freeze, Dale left the bar. And left Anna.

HE'S BEEN BACK HOME a year now, and it's been six months since he stopped checking the mailbox compulsively. He has no idea if news would come in a letter in any case. That was just romantic, archaic. If word from her ever comes, it would be her voice on the phone, a simple "Now what?" Or it might be email, just as flippant, the subject line "Geoffrey Firmin Needs Money." He hasn't seen her for a year. She might be dead. Though he doubts that. But she might be anything at all.

He sees that he now thinks of her fondly. It helps him with the troubling times, though you'd think it would be the opposite. When he pictures her she's usually swimming in the pool, there in Conchas Chinas, while he watches her from up on their balcony, where he stands slightly frightened, two feet back from the railing, not touching it and leaning forward to peer over. She wasn't a fluid swimmer and the punchiness of her stroke was somehow juvenile, and oddly sexy for it. He was perched three storeys above, so if he called her up for a sandwich or she cajoled him into joining her, they had to shout. The time he remembers most was when Anna, on the poolside lounger reading his Carlos Castaneda book, suddenly dropped it, unfinished and unbookmarked, beside her onto the concrete, done. It looked like she'd read maybe twenty pages. She dropped the book sadly, gently, maybe because she knew she was dropping something dear to him. He witnessed the whole thing. It was the third book in the series. He really should have brought the first one for her, because it did a better job of preparing for the wise insanity that followed. The third book assumed a lot, too much. So maybe it was his fault. In any case she dropped the book and stared off, her sadness continuing, probably deepening, at what she saw to be the naivety of the man she'd married. Then she looked up. He doesn't know if she already knew he was up there watching. But she looked up, saw him, tapped the dropped book with a finger and shouted, funny and sad both, "Come on." And then, "Really?"

She knew that he wanted it to be true. She knew that he respected its instructions on how to live, on how to hunt life's hidden purpose. How to *see*. When Anna dropped the book, there was nothing of her feeling superior. Nor was she sad for him. She was sad for them, this much was clear. She hopped up from her lounger then and, without another word, dived in. Whenever she wanted to feel better, Anna jumped into water, went for a fresh walk or uncapped a bottle.

They did try. She'd also brought *Under the Volcano*, for him. He'd been sitting up there on the balcony with it resting on his lap. Heavy as hell and intimidating. Likely because he was trying to read it only for her, he found it impenetrable. And in the end, despite the colourful self-torture of Firmin drinking himself to death, surrounded by spiky Mexican exotica, it was boring. Let's call a spade a spade. In any case, the two books only proved how wrong they had been to think that the two Mexicos they'd imagined might be remotely the same country.

"Why do you hate me right now? Right this second?" was the last thing he'd asked Anna, there in that bar, in J's Corruption. He'd stood watching her dance, by herself, for two songs. Her unabashed style wasn't unlike her swimming. Using her body to get a job done. At the start of the third song, a well-built guy, white shirt so tight that Dale suspected he was Mexican, joined her. No conversation, but their chests stayed pointed at each other through the dance, George Thorogood's "Bad to the Bone," which made Dale snicker through his nose as he hurried out. He had no evidence that she'd ever cheated on him, and he didn't want evidence now. On his way out he stopped in the *banyo*. As he peed, something smelled wonderful. He looked up to see vanilla beans—that is, the long black pods—maybe a dozen of them, dangling from the ceiling, just out of jumping reach. He remembers that, angry as he was, he realized right away that the women's *banyo* would have them too, and so he'd wondered, when Anna did visit the *banyo*, what she would think of them. She'd instantly see the contradiction between their look and their smell. She would call them God's little shits, or something like that. Something wittier and better. Satan's dreams.

He doesn't know if she came back to their villa that night, after J's, because he didn't go back himself. Technically, he left her more than she left him. Two days later, when he did return to their villa, he timed things for when the maid would be going through it, so if Anna was around she'd be down at the pool. Dale didn't go to the balcony to check because he didn't want to know. Nor could he tell if the bed had been slept in because it was already made. There was no scatter of empty bottles, but they might have been cleaned up. He noticed a new birdcage, of ornate bamboo wicker. The fruit bowl was full of green papayas and the small, wrinkled yellow mangos she loved. He nodded to the shyly smiling but perplexed maid, stuffed his clothes into his suitcase and taxied to his new room on the modern, less colourful side of town.

The next afternoon Dale saw Anna for the last time. He encountered her by accident, on the Malecon boardwalk. It had been their favourite haunt, so he shouldn't have been walking there in the first place. He didn't know what he was up to—maybe he wanted to see her. Maybe he wanted to grab her back and protect her from everything, especially herself. Maybe she wanted him to, and maybe he knew that. He'd even got badly drunk, in a bar by himself, the night before, telling himself he was doing it in sympathy, in communal spirit, sharing that magical expansion, that wise loving embrace that alcohol can sometimes extend. It was in the darkest corner of the seediest bar he could find, no English to be heard anywhere, and on a windowsill he saw a dirty brown lizard that made him laugh and swear and point, and some *macho caballero* shouted something at him, and Dale may actually have been in danger, even as he turned to him and smiled dumbly and shrugged. All that kept him from going off in search of Anna that night was his staggering state—he felt certain he was embracing her in any case with his own Lowry drunkenness, and he felt certain she'd wait for him every night at J's Corruption, because that's what forlorn lovers did.

But when he saw her that next afternoon on the Malecon, she wasn't drunk. Dale followed at a distance. He noted bracelets and bangles, silver, stacked up both wrists. She was carrying a bouquet of dyed feathers in the most garish colours. She wore a new peasant blouse, that unbleached cotton. She appeared pretty much carefree. She wasn't looking for anyone, for anyone at all—that was clear enough. Every twenty seconds or so Dale mumbled "No, *gracias*" to the latest vendor shaking a trinket or T-shirt in his face, and he watched her strategy for handling the same. She had the pockets of her shorts pulled out, and to turn down a vendor she shook her bangled silver wrists at him and then pointed to her empty pockets, smiling. She had a phrase or two to share with each, and to a man they laughed back and left her alone.

Leaving the Malecon, after several blocks she entered a café called the Blue Shrimp. The way she turned in to it, without looking, told him she'd been there before. He waited outside long enough to hear her say something in Spanish, hear something said back—a clutch of women it sounded like—and then Anna laughed as loud as Dale had heard her laugh in years.

He realized what was different about her. She had the look of someone who hadn't had a drink in three days. The exact amount of time since she'd last laid eyes on him. She looked uncomplicated, and fresh. She looked free of both of them.

NO, SHE'S NOT DEAD, though they do say it's either all or nothing for people like her. It's not a case of being smart or stupid. Lowry was a genius, as Anna never ceased pointing out. It all might just be luck. Or who your companions are.

But what's she doing? He doesn't know what she's thinking right now, doesn't have a clue. He suspects that their famous fatal intimacy was bullshit all along. How could he not have a clue? He opened new bank accounts but kept their old joint account with enough in it to keep her going awhile, though the two times he peeked it hadn't been touched, and he's since forced himself to stop looking. He knows she would have had to come north to get her visa renewed by now. So likely she's been in town. She might still be. Her work never did call, nor did any of her friends—so they all must know, and they must have been given instructions. He takes nothing from this; it could mean love or it could mean hate, and isn't that funny? Mostly what it means is confusion, because that is their epitaph. In any case, he bets he's not far off when he pictures her wearing something colourful—turquoise, rose, yellow—and giving lessons of some sort, maybe working in that café where he heard her laugh. Keeping up a simple, clean, one-room place. Keeping birds. He sees her as someone he'd like to meet, and take walks with. Have adventures.

Dale was back home more than two months before he noticed the *Speak Spanish!* book. He was in the process of packing everything up to move to a smaller apartment, because a single man does not need two bathrooms, and he found one with a decent view from the balcony, a silver-blue glimpse of Burrard Inlet up through to Indian Arm, which, irony of ironies, was where Lowry lived when he wrote *Volcano.* (Delighted, as speechless as a little girl, Anna had taken him along to explore Lowry Walk, a surprisingly serene path through beachfront forest.)

Dale found the bright red *Speak Spanish!* book in the small bathroom, as they used to call it. The book was sitting plain as day on the back of the toilet where she'd left it, ready for her to pick up and commit one or two more words to memory. As soon as he saw it he realized he'd seen it quite a bit, lying around the place. He thinks he saw Anna prone on the couch reading it, saying words aloud, trying her accent, excited for their vacation and boning up for it—but to tell the truth, she was right, he hadn't been paying attention. None at all.

Only since finding the book had he begun to see the size of his mistake.

Now every few days he opens her closet to check her clothes, feeling the fabric, trying to remember her wearing this blouse or those jeans. Sometimes he can. But these clothes of hers, which was everything she chose not to bring to Mexico, feel like cast-offs, and part of what she'd happily left behind.

Black
Roses
Bloom

Sharing his pillow, Katherine asks if it's ever happened to him. Redmond goes up on an elbow. His sandy hair is mussed and boyish, despite the high, intelligent forehead. She finds exotic the permanent snarl of his lips, and that trace of English accent flips her heart.

"Never. That's never happened to me, Kath."

Even lying naked beside him, Katherine finds it hard to talk about sex. She'll use timid hand gestures, or resort to the worst euphemisms. Your peter. My—he laughs at this one—nether region. Redmond is the first man with whom she's talked about it. This morning they have ten minutes to linger before they must shower, dress and drive to the bank where they work.

What's happened is, she mentioned the flood of dreams she had at her orgasm, and he was surprised.

Katherine adds, "Lately it's happening even more. Maybe every time. Should I be worried?"

Redmond presses a knuckle into her shoulder and lies back on his pillow. "Well, I'm jealous. I don't even get to have my pillow-smoke anymore." Redmond quit smoking at her insistence a week after they met (just as he got her to quit her glasses for contact lenses). Though it's been three months he jokes about it constantly, slyly blaming. One thing he says is, Europeans are elegant smokers, so they should be allowed to.

Redmond asks her, more softly, "So what exactly did you see today? In your post-coital reverie."

Katherine tells him it's hard to describe because it's a flood, a stream, of random images. But little stories too. The main thing is, it feels like memory. It's dreams she's had before. Lots, she's certain, are from her childhood.

"So I'm not *having* them," she says, understanding it more herself. "I'm *remembering* them." All feel drenched in nostalgia. The sweetness of long-lost.

"Give us an example, then." Said like a plucky English schoolmaster. Hello, Mr. Chips.

Mostly Katherine is afraid of boring him. She knows she's stiff; she knows she's not colourful. If there's one thing she's afraid of with Redmond, it's that. And aren't people famously bored by others' dreams? She'll keep it short.

"One was, I'm in a pet store. There's a goldfish, it becomes the dog I always wanted, and I think as we're walking home, it turns brown and gets old and dies." Back on the pillow, Redmond stares straight up, blinking. She says, "And one I was in China, that place with the craggy mountains rising out of the water, and I fling myself off this cliff, because apparently I can fly, since I had this secret training. But I just fall into the trees. I'm completely embarrassed, because I was bragging about flying to all these tourists. Chinese tourists. I try to fall deeper into the branches so they can't see me anymore."

"Wow," Redmond whispers. He may in fact have said "Oh." He's either bored or concerned.

Katherine can't help herself.

"And there's this pineapple I pick, and it's full of wonderfully cooked meat. A stew, a curry. It's spiced like heaven. There's gold *nuggets* shining up from it. Then there's this ceremony for me ..."

"This happens every time you cum?"

At first she thinks he means does a ceremony happen every time. And she so dislikes that word, cum. He somehow even pronounces its abbreviated spelling.

"Maybe. Yes."

He smiles. "It's usually the man who does the passing out." He looks sideways at her, vast brow furrowed. "You actually do pass out?"

Katherine simply nods. She's already explained that she does. She wants to ask other things, wants to know that she's not some kind of freak. Is she too loud, or not loud enough? Or would he like her to resist a little at first, or maybe he'd like to be stroked after, in "the afterglow"? Part of which she spends stricken by dreams.

Redmond squeezes her knee and is first up and into the shower. Her revelation seems to have made him quiet, but then he's humming in the spray. Katherine can smell a waft of her shampoo, which he doesn't mind using. Lately he's been staying over two, sometimes three nights a week, and there's been mention of finding a place together. She's fond of her condo and proud that it's mortgage-free, and though it will hurt to lose it, it's necessary that they find *their* place. They have yet to discuss her equity and his lack of same. But—as Redmond might joke as they divide a restaurant check—they're both bankers, this shouldn't be hard.

REDMOND LOVES ME. Katherine can say this and does daily, aloud to herself, in smiling amazement. She is forty-five and had almost given up on that part of her life—the relationship part, the love part. Over the years she'd worked at two ragged and prolonged affairs, but until Redmond, there wasn't love. She'd even begun telling herself that this part of life, the love part, didn't really matter, almost convincing herself that since you're born alone and die alone, the long middle part would only be muddled by a partner. Loneliness, she'd been whispering to herself, built character. She sees now that in life's bruising race to the finish line, she's been positioning pillows between herself and her greatest pain. But now Redmond loves her—she's sure of it— and she loves Redmond, and there's nothing muddled about it. Their love is a sentence that began clear and continues clear. The orgasms, the first in her life, are magical punctuation. Are proof.

THAT NIGHT: A FLAME-GREEN BIRD, its song the *tink* of a cheap souvenir bell and poignant for it. Then her father's face in the side window of a black car, a criminal's car. He sees her, points at her, laughs behind glass. She's on the weedy sidewalk in front of her childhood house. A long-forgotten truth: the smell of her trike tires.

RESTLESS IN THE WAITING ROOM, Katherine almost gets up to leave. Magazine beauty ads can't distract her. Her horoscope in the back is spectacularly good and says her love will grow, but she reads the others too and they're all spectacular and apparently good love is everywhere, which she knows is garbage. She feels foolish coming here and doubts a family doctor would know anything about orgasm dreams anyway. But last week, before Redmond's special dinner for her, she promised herself she'd get it checked if it happened again despite her efforts to stop it. They ate the Sicilian macaroni, finished the wine while listening to the wily jazz Redmond had brought, moved to the bedroom, enjoyed sex—after the peak of which she sank instantly into dreams. In that way of dreams, she was aware of herself having them but at the same times helpless to stop: she's beside a beautiful glacial river, with a smell of dry, hot pine needles, it's Banff, she's barefoot and shouldn't be, she's lost her shoes and is hunting for them. Then mostly it's glimpses—like thumbing through colour swatches—whiffs of emotions that by turns tug, gladden, make restless. They all feel like memory.

In her inner office Dr. Reynolds asks awkward questions. Katherine would prefer being physically naked to this. Dr. Reynolds is roughly Katherine's age and her name is Dorothy, but despite knowing her for two decades, Katherine has never been invited to call her that. Which is fine, especially now.

"So let's clarify. Sexually—you've never had orgasms before. Not even through self-stimulation."

Katherine nods, won't meet her eye. So let's clarify my freakishness.

"And, the effort it takes. To reach orgasm. You say it's lots of work. So can you tell me, out of ten, with ten being the highest, how much effort it takes?"

"I didn't mean it's just work. I don't know quite what—"

"Of course it's 'enjoyable.'" Dr. Reynolds does quotation marks and almost smiles. Imagining this thick woman in the crisp smock having orgasms too, Katherine doesn't know if it's endearing or nauseating. The doctor continues, "But, subtracting the enjoyment, can you describe the effort? Is it distressing? Do you ever feel faint or—"

"Ten. It's ten." But an enjoyable ten. Please, Dorothy, shut up. She will not describe herself at her peak. She will tell no one that she is desperate to burst but can't, and that what it often takes in the end is Redmond saying her name, with his low voice, his accent, and it is proof of their love that he could know this.

TODAY, A SATURDAY MORNING, Katherine is extra self-conscious. She's in the middle of telling Redmond three lies. First—a lie of omission—she's not told him what her doctor wants her to do the next time they make love. Second, she's told Redmond that her dripping faucet is driving her crazy, she thinks it's just a washer, will he please, please come over and fix it, she even has tools and an extra washer—when in fact she opened the faucet herself and purposely mangled the washer with a pair of pliers.

Redmond arrives, game to try, looking annoyed but proud, she can tell, to have been asked. He's cute in his plaid workshirt, which looks brand new, perhaps bought right after her phone call, and it's also cute that he's deemed such a shirt necessary. She hands him several wrenches, hoping he will be able to figure out the right one—he does—and she drops just enough advice while watching him fix her faucet.

When Redmond finishes, one knuckle is bleeding. He taps the faucet and, so English, announces, "Right," and tries the taps. He's slightly amazed and then proud of the water gushing into the basin.

She hands him a coffee to sip while she tries hot, then cold, cooing amazement too. Katherine's not a good actor, but she takes his collar in both hands and says, "My hero," coy as Marilyn Monroe. She adds, "There's something about a man and his tools," the line made lamer for being pre-planned, and declares that she can't let him leave without giving him his reward. This, the third lie, she knows won't stay a lie. His work clothes and clumsiness hadn't been arousing at all, but once in bed she knows she'll rise to the occasion. She takes Redmond by the hand, senses reluctance and, Marilyn again, tilts her head to undo the buttons over his chest. Redmond asks if it's this Bob the Builder shirt that's caught her eye, and she says, yes, it's *absolutely unbearable*, joining his joke. And Katherine sees how love can deepen even in lies and frivolity.

All part of the plan, she must have him gone by two because the clinic closes at three. Dr. Reynolds wants Katherine tested within an hour of having sex. That is, of having an orgasm. That is, of being stricken with dreams. In her office, face falling professionally soft, Dr. Dorothy had told Katherine that the brain releases an enzyme into the blood when part of it dies. The blood test will be for a stroke.

Today, after the faucet repair: She's on a plane, a propeller plane, and there's turbulence. The pilot sings to them in what sounds Mexican, then becomes Irish. The plane isn't falling yet, but everyone seems to know it's about to. She's the only one afraid, though she isn't really, and her screams are insincere, though she tries her best to make them real. As the plane's nose tilts down and things speed up, the woman in the seat to her left dares her, hands her a knife. And from Katherine's wrist black roses bloom.

SUCH IS THEIR LOVE that they don't discuss much. She doesn't understand men, but she and Redmond seem to share a knowing. She is sure of it. They haven't, for instance, had to speak of work, where she's branch manager and he occupies an echelon or two below. Redmond jokes about his smaller office and salary—in the parking lot he once shouted across to her, *At least my car is bigger.* They both know that he entered the financial world late, and that he is capable and might keep climbing. None of this needs to be mentioned. And though Katherine yearns to proclaim their love, would proudly arrive at work hand in hand, they both know to keep it hidden due to the perception that their relationship might be advantageous for him. She knows there likely are odious murmurs that he is sleeping his way up the ladder. But he can joke about this too. It felt dangerous, it felt almost like sex, when he surprised her that time in bed, announcing deadpan, "If you promote me I'll marry you." When he left it at that, unexplained, she lay there paralyzed for the longest time, until finally he coughed out laughter, and then she joined him, desperately and with relief that they *were* laughing, she feeling like a dry well suddenly filling with water, the sweetest, warmest water. It brimmed in her eyes. She could see that Redmond knew just how dangerous he was to her. And he knew that she knew, and they didn't need to say a word.

KATHERINE UNDRESSES FOR BED. Redmond is in the living room, comfortable in her recliner, enjoying a magazine article on the Vancouver Island mountain lion. She half-listens as he explains to her loudly from the other room that the big cat was bounty-hunted and almost wiped out, and that only the fiercest survived to breed, which is why there are more attacks on Vancouver Island than the rest of North America combined. She slides into bed with her book. He will join her eventually, and even if he has to wake her, they will make love. When he sleeps over, they have never not made love.

She is scheduled at the hospital next week for a strange procedure involving electrodes, shaved head and more. It also involves a vibrator and an orgasm. She knows she won't go through with it. She simply won't show up. She would be alone in a room, but her pleasure, as well as her blackout and her dreams, would appear onscreen as angry red or glaring green, indicating bleeding or oxygen or a shrieking lack of it, all to be interpreted by men in long smocks. Ever since the blood tests proclaimed the worst—a series of small strokes—and a neurologist confirmed the losses in brain function, Katherine has paid more attention to the dreams. They have grown precious to her. How could they not? She imagines each brain cell as a vault that holds a single image and blooms proudly with it as it dies. They have her on blood thinners. She has been told to avoid stress and exercise, especially sex, sex most of all, since this is what, mysteriously, is killing her.

Redmond enters her bedroom yawning grandly, head kinked against shoulder, arms flung out, hands in fists. Katherine pretends to read. Her body is minutely shaking. He loves her. How has she managed to do this? He will interrupt her reading with a loving hand on her shoulder.

Soon enough, he does. His lips are on her neck, he is humming a jazzy non-melody and warmth thrills up her spine, forcing her eyes closed. All her life, all her life, she has waited.

TONIGHT A PERFECT PIE cools on a cottage windowsill, as in a fairy tale. The dream itself knows it's corny. The crust she pushes open with a finger, and it smells like fruit and meat combined, a deep genius of food. She eats it as she walks a forest path. Then falls off the cliff that surprises her, though she knows she's fallen off it before. She watches herself falling. She looks at her hands. She makes herself fall slower so she can study her hands. She can flex them. Amazing: she can grow those fingernails, can watch her fingernails growing. The dream goes on and on, as dreams are willing to do.

At Work
in the Fields
of the
Bulwer-Lytton

H is sister's phone call interrupted him composing his next bad sentence:

His loincloth coming away with the sound of low-grade adhesive

Raymond let Elizabeth talk. When she was done, he dropped his phone from a height and with a noise that made him check for cracked plastic. He couldn't take it anymore. Leaning back in his chair he balanced on the two rear legs to the verge of toppling. He had learned not to hear the muffled booming of pucks in the six rinks outside his office's glass door, but he heard them now. He moaned low and long, building it nearly to a shout. As always, he was damned if he said something and damned if he didn't. After a week's research, his sister, fifty-three, was convinced not only of having Alzheimer's, but a particularly swift kind that attacked the young. His sincerely intentioned comment—that if she had Alzheimer's she couldn't have done such excellent research on Alzheimer's—had caused her to announce, "You just abandoned me," and hang up.

He didn't know what to do. It hurt to think about. Because he loved her, he supposed.

Raymond let his chair fall forward. He picked up his pencil. She'd be crying now. The one upside to these more explosive conversations was that she wouldn't call him for a week. Unless ... she forgot. No, he mustn't make light of this. Maybe she did display more memory loss of late, more than just the name-forgetting kind, and both their parents had gone daffy before they died. But her panic was unbearable. Today asking him, all a-fever, if she should check her iron levels again, because they can point to arterial blockage and oxygen depletion in— Her voice was shaking and what's he supposed to say?

Raymond never panicked. It dismayed him that his older sister could be so different in this way. They were only two years apart. They had the same curly ginger hair, the same swelling cheekbones with unfortunate small eyes. They were both high-strung and made impractical life decisions. Their tastes were so similar that it didn't surprise him, for instance, to learn that Elizabeth disliked Chilean wine, and that her reasons were exactly his.

Shaking his head minutely, in the kind of spasm that did mean to abandon his sister for a week, Raymond leaned over his foolscap to read his latest. This was the best time of year, these spring weeks leading up to the deadline. He finished reading it, hesitated, then pencil-tapped it with approval. Fixing a few circled bits as he went, he committed this to his computer screen:

*His loincloth coming away with the sound of a low-grade
adhesive, Jungle Jones eyed his next conquest, tried and
failed to grunt like one of his idols, a silverback, rose to his
feet and leapt to the liana vine, from which he fell because
he was tired from all the conquesting.*

It wasn't his best but it was a keeper he'd enter in the
Romance category, under one of his pseudonyms. Marvin Gets.
Westley Winns. Thomas Smother. It was Thomas Smother
who won a dishonourable mention two years ago in the Crime
category. Raymond had that one committed to memory:

*As they lay waiting in the alley, involuntarily spooning, for
the thugs to run past, his overcoat could not cushion him
from the press of her Luger, which made his own gun feel
like nothing but a Mauser in his belt—because that's all he
had, a lousy Mauser—so he was glad his back was to her.*

He could recall the spreading glow in his stomach when he
was notified. He remembered how surprised he'd been that this
one had won; it was nowhere near the best of the thirty or so
he'd submitted that year—and the contest itself dissuaded the
use of the dash.

He copied his sentence into the body of a new email and
popped Send, nostalgic for the days when it was done by letter.
One entry per envelope. Stamps did get expensive, but everything about good old mail—the labour of addressing, the
folding of paper and the taste of glue, the frisky walk in all

kinds of weather to the mailbox, not to mention the primal act of sliding a letter through a spring-loaded slot—all of it suited the contest's archaic soul. Apparently there was a torrent of complaints when the rules changed.

This year Raymond's goal was one hundred entries. He was at fifty-seven. He no longer cared much if he won. The goal was the path.

AS ON-SITE MANAGER of ArenaSix, Raymond was content enough with his job, it being understood here that work was work and one would rather be elsewhere. He kept the ice sheets near to booked and resurfaced between sessions, the two Zambonis in repair, the monthly schedules publicized, the bar/restaurant staffed with nubiles (as Nabokov had called them), and the hockey parents away from the throats of the parents of figure skaters (though the skaters' parents, especially the mothers, tended as a species to be the fiercest and most blind to compromise). And though his job also oversaw the losing battle to keep beer out of the changing rooms during men's late-night hockey, it was, as jobs went, not unbearable.

Though on occasion he had to fire someone. This morning it was Mr. Fernandez, one of his two maintenance men. Through his damnable glass door Raymond had been eyeing Mr. Fernandez perched out there on the bench, waiting in the cold. No one should have to wait in the cold on a bench like that one, wooden and skate-mauled, let alone someone about to be fired. Raymond was further disappointed that the man hadn't had the good graces to come alone. As always, he'd brought Paytro (likely the name was Pedro, but it always sounded like "Paytro"), as if he didn't know his son was the heart of the problem. Paytro had Down syndrome, was perhaps in his adolescence and never stopped fidgeting, especially a grand rolling of one hand around the axis of his wrist. The boy held his twirling hand out from his body in a way that suggested ritual, and because each roll made the faintest click, Raymond guessed that the patrons of this place were as nauseated by this as he was. Despite two warnings, Mr. Fernandez insisted, intermittently at first and then always, on bringing Paytro with him to work.

Raymond re-read his sentence. He turned off the screen.

He stood, stretched, then opened the door to Mr. Fernandez, who ushered wrist-rolling Paytro in first.

The whole affair was predictably uncomfortable. Mr. Fernandez nodded when asked if he knew why he was being called in, and then he demanded that Raymond explain things to his son.

"I would like to hear you say to Paytro why we are not wanted anymore" is how the glowering maintenance man put it.

Why explain what Fernandez already knew, that the problem was the "we"? Fernandez had proved an excellent painter, cleaner and, most of all, fixer. In the shop he'd used a grinding machine to shape a piece of scrap metal that somehow fixed the number two Zamboni. The problem was solely the "we." Paytro was never not with him. More and more, Fernandez gave him jobs to do. Sometimes, the father simply stood watching the son sweep or rake or polish.

"Your son gets in the way of you doing the job you were hired to—"

"Say this to Paytro. Look at him when you say it."

Now Fernandez was only being cruel. Fine.

"Paytro, I've asked your father to come to work alone, and he refuses. I've asked him formally, twice. We call them warnings. He ignores—"

"Tell Paytro why you want me to work alone."

"Fine." Raymond swung his gaze back to the son. The boy watched him back. He was hard to read. It was hard to know what he understood. "Your father is a good worker, a highly skilled worker, and that is what we pay—"

It came out shouted, sloppy, but with equal emphasis on each word: *"I'm a good worker too."*

"Yes, but—"

"He's teaching me."

What struck Raymond most was the boy's utter lack of accent, considering his father's was so thick. Paytro had hidden his twirl-hand in his windbreaker and it humped around in there, shushing the nylon. Raymond recalled times he'd spied on Fernandez as he supervised Paytro scrubbing solvent on puck marks or, outside, sweeping the leaf-blower in scythe-like arcs. Fernandez would interrupt and take over his son's slow job, demonstrating proper pace, then hand back the gear. Raymond suspected that the father-son team was productive enough to justify Fernandez's salary. It was that he'd been told to come alone and he'd blatantly ignored the order. A boss could not just ignore being ignored. In a hierarchy, insurrection created consequences. It was nothing but natural, and Raymond must let nature take its course.

He spoke clearly and met Paytro's eye.

"You are a good worker. I am glad he is teaching you. But, as manager, I have to end your father's employment here. The reason? I told him to come to work alone, and he didn't obey me. I told him twice. Then I told him three times."

Looking at Fernandez, he once again explained that insurance didn't cover his son, who, if hurt, could sue both of them. Surprising himself, Raymond added that, once fired, Fernandez could apply again for his job. Finally, he said he could supply him with a good reference letter if he wanted, but Fernandez was already shaking his head in automatic disbelief and leaving, guiding Paytro out the door ahead of him.

But first Fernandez stopped, turned to face Raymond, ponderously held his eyes to say, in his heavy accent, "Look at youself," then left.

Raymond respected Fernandez enough to do this, so he sat down. The instructive silence grew louder with the man gone. He sat with this task for several minutes, then flipped open his laptop. It was likely the start of another entry for Romance:

"An unexamined life," she said, naked of irony as well as clothing,

He saved it and closed his machine. Raymond had learned that when he memorized an opening fragment and then went about his day, some part of his brain kept working behind the scenes and came up with the best bad ideas.

Down an employee, he had to scrape and flood three ice surfaces himself. It was a chore he found more meditative than anything else, though skaters did complain, especially the old-timer hockey players, who demanded the most pristine surface, like they were fairies of the pond, not chuggers. But he couldn't quite find the knack, or settings, and he left grooves. He wished he could have accelerated hiring a new man, but you couldn't very well advertise before firing, could you?

> *"An unexamined life," she said, naked of irony as well as clothing,*

Riding high on the Zamboni, he let phrases simmer as he drove an oddly rectangular oval, old mauled snow disappearing under the front bumper while a strip of shining water followed. He tried to work up more:

> *as they rode together on the Zamboni, its engine beneath their bare, cold bottoms droning deeply but blindly, like a massive phallus asleep but prowling in its dream*

Bad-on-purpose was anything but easy. It had to be knowingly salacious. It had to be subtle in its build to looniness. (He mentally crossed out the massive-phallus-asleep line, which was somehow both too cheap and too poetic.) Clauses had to invert and sometimes buckle and then flow horribly on.

Clichés had to be the right ones. Puns were discouraged unless they stretched pun-logic to snapping. And were punishing! The best entries tended to rise in a limp frenzy and end not on a punchline but on a downbeat, like tobacco spittle after a hillbilly whoop—which was how it might indeed be described in Bulwer-Lytton language. It was a near-impossible contest to win, with its thousands upon thousands of entries. This despite no cash award at all. Crime, Western, Science Fiction, Romance, Historical Fiction, Fantasy—all categories had their aficionados, their style-mavens. Sometimes Raymond recognized the entrants before reading their names.

Cruising rink number three he came upon another bit. After parking and shutting down (he simply left the snow to sit and melt in the Zamboni's back bin instead of dumping it outside; Bernie was on in an hour and he'd do that chore, grumbling and swearing), he hurried back upstairs to type:

"An unexamined life," she said, naked of both irony and clothing, as they rode atop the Zamboni, its engine beneath their bare, cold bottoms droning deeply but blindly in its work, which when you thought of it was nothing but eating snow at the front and spraying water out the back, "is

Is what. Nothing more came. He opened a new file. He was hungry, and it was almost time to go, but he had a palpable sense of time running out. It was getting down to the wire. He stood hovering over the keyboard, shifting foot to foot on his office's weird rubber floor, stepping in and out of two pools of water under his shoes. It wasn't just taking a good idea one bad step too far. It was rhythm too; it was building a good sentence with a tin-ear clunk that sabotaged it.

After ten minutes he had this:

Her heart's desire ran in two directions, the main one leading to her husband, the other to Jungle Jones, but her lust ran in even more directions, so many that the word "direction" lost all meaning, like when you said it over and over, say, a hundred or, in her case, seven hundred and sixty-three times.

Raymond had no idea who the hell Jungle Jones was, what he looked like or what readers—if there were any—made of the name. It just sounded right. It was funny in that slightly gut-churning way.

He pressed Send. Submitting entries he knew wouldn't win felt a bit like throwing letters at a closed mailbox. Or, like pissing at a tree protected by glass! He typed "is like pissing on a tree protected behind glass" at the end of "An unexamined life." He read it a couple of times. Then deleted it. It was too abstract, however astute it might be philosophically.

He was closing his laptop, anticipating his nicer screen at home, when the phone rang. Elizabeth's bouts of solitary depression usually lasted awhile, plus she did tend to respect his request not to call him at work, so he was surprised it was her a second time this afternoon. Her tone of saying hello told him she was beyond instructing, so he kept censure from his voice when he told her how nice it was to hear from her again today. She ignored him—interrupted him, in fact—and what she said sat him up straight.

"Raymond. I want to kill myself, sooner rather than later, and I want your help."

"My help. To …"

"To do it, yes."

He could picture the musty brown couch she was probably sitting on, its fabric a reminder of haunted theatres, and it made him sadder than her words had. He asked her to repeat herself, and she did so, word for word, including his name with the period after it, as if to make sure he knew he could not escape.

After the call Raymond sat for a while. He neither moved nor intended to. Pucks boomed without meaning outside his door. He promised himself he would not feel guilt when he opened his laptop. When he did, he typed this:

> *Jungle Jane wasn't given to cheap sentiment, but she wondered, fingering the noose around her neck, test-rocking the rickety chair beneath her feet, thinking disturbedly of the empty pill bottles scattered like Hansel's bread crusts along the sidewalk all the way to her house, if he would still respect her tomorrow.*

WITH THE DEADLINE creeping ever closer, Raymond finished thirty-eight more sentences over the next weeks, taking him to ninety-six. Five he considered exceptional, with a solid chance at a prize or a mention. He'd been coming to work distracted. He wrestled awkward phrases in his dreams, and a good dangling modifier could wake him. He was afflicted by sentences whose skewed meaning wouldn't leave. "The hole in her cheek, larger than her head ..." always made him try to visualize it, and then he had to stand up, breathe and run on the spot. One Saturday night he stayed up till dawn and one day he slept in and was an hour late for work, two things that had never happened before. He stopped taking Elizabeth's calls and she did try to kill herself, half-heartedly and without his help, displaying both her indecision and impatience in this as in all things. Since taking up residence in the psych ward she seemed more stoically content than she had in years. She was proud to have improved at Sudoku and she thought her memory disease was getting better, but Raymond didn't think so and suspected it was just the structured regimen of hospital life, though of course he said nothing. He lost half of the pinky finger of his left hand while trying to adjust the height ratchet of the scraper under the number two Zamboni, and now it hurt like the devil to type, but almost a ghost pain, because his pinky never had touched keys in the first place and it certainly didn't now. Several times he saw Paytro out on the main street near the arena complex, quite alone, walking steadily as if pulled by the propeller of his rotating hand. Mr. Fernandez didn't reapply for his job, though Raymond continued to wish he had, because MacLean, the new fellow he'd hired, scared him with a latent insubordination so severe he thought it could someday become violent. Maybe it was the prison tattoos on the knuckles of MacLean's hand, "JESUS" or not, the "J" almost unrecognizable there on the thumb. The man made good ice, but he could barely bring himself to nod when Raymond wished him a good morning or nice weekend. So Raymond stopped saying these things.

And God knows why, but tonight, the night of the deadline and with four more entries to make one hundred, he went on the date he'd found excuses to put off for months and months. It was his first date in easily a dozen years, more like fifteen and perhaps closer to twenty. It had also been that long since he'd had sex. It was in the back of his mind that, yes, he was probably giving it one last chance. Not just romance, but everything, anything. Her name was Leslie and she lived on the same floor; theirs had been an elevator relationship since she moved in. She was shy to the point of being monosyllabic. He suspected correctly that it would make her even more nervous, but because he never went out himself he took her to an absurdly high-end seafood place that had recently opened, called only small "s," a simple unlit woodblock affixed to the concrete wall. (Apparently the famous chef's previous restaurant had been called "sea.") He could tell that one part of her wanted to make some kind of racy joke out of ordering the raw oysters appetizer but she couldn't bring herself to do it. Instead she ate them non-theatrically and embarrassed. In a kind of answer to her non-delivered joke he picked up an oyster body with his injured hand, the bandage only recently off, knowing it would look ugly, and he positioned it to his ear and knit his brow for a few seconds, then simply laid it back in its open shell, not saying, "Listening for pearls." He made a promise with himself that if she was sensitive enough to know exactly what he'd just done, and what his joke had been, he would ask her to marry him. But she pretended not to have seen him do it. The food was very good, in some sense too good, and they spoke respectfully about each different dish, and the wine. That and careful politics, from which he could gather that she was the more liberal. He knew he could have sex if he wanted, but he didn't. Nor did he want to analyze why.

After he stumbled over her name while saying goodnight outside their elevator like always, he got home, turned on his computer and read items from his favourite news sources. Headlines abounded concerning what some were calling "the most perfect storm," wherein UN reports of irrefutable proof that ocean levels would indeed rise combined with several countries colluding to default on their debt, which appeared to be nudging global markets past anarchy toward total collapse. Next, he read local weather forecasts. Any dramatic change in temperatures meant he needed to adjust settings at work, for ice conditions. The next week appeared stable.

Raymond opened his files, found the sentence and typed:

"An unexamined life," she said, cold naked ironic bum blah blah, "is like keeping wings tucked, is like staying in the nest, is like staying in the egg, is like never being born."

Thus completing that problem sentence. Which, for reasons too obvious to think about, he didn't send.

Midnight was the deadline. He did reach ninety-nine, typing three more in a final flurry, sitting there at his laptop, sweating, good clothes still on and pinching at the throat and crotch, sentences that had been percolating throughout dinner.

These he wrote without strategizing much, bad sentences a good habit now, and after fixing a single punctuation error he considered them finished and pressed Send three final times. He deemed them neither good nor bad, because you couldn't tell anymore, you truly couldn't. Especially in recent years, when even irony was used ironically, when bland-on-purpose square-danced with cool. Not that these were that.

In the restaurant so fancy it had no name at all, never blinking at him once, she slowly slurped several slippery bivalves in an attempt to seduce him, which eventually would have worked, had she not had to pay a visit to the little girls' room, where she sauntered to, to vomit.

"Well, if it's grizzly bears you're after," Jungle Jane lisped at him from the dank, musky cavity of her cabin window, batting her one eyelash as she did, because one of her eyes lacked a lid, having been sliced off sometime during the squirrel-roast, "why don't you just head round to my backyard and shoot one?"

It was the final climatic enormity whose name no one dared breathe, the news of which struck terror in the hearts of all men, and animals too, and even some fish, for though they generally lived underwater, and lacked ears, they could pick up on the hubbub and general nervousness of all the humans and animals stomping around in terror up here, especially on the beach.

Four
Corners

Jack decides, again. Tonight's the night.

He drains his wine, a favourite pinot noir that tastes thin this evening, gets up to pour another and brings the bottle back to the couch with him. This doesn't have to be painful, Cheryl won't necessarily make a scene. She is reasonable. Which is maybe part of the problem. But you never know with reasonable types. And hell hath no fury like. He *can* conceive of Cheryl throwing something. He can also see a lolling sadness, and he wonders if that wouldn't be harder to take.

She's in her bathroom standing in front of the mirror and he can see parts of her only when an elbow shoots out or she tosses that beautiful hair of hers. She's using a very throwable brush to pull through it, the one vanity she indulges, despite or perhaps because she's not far from getting too old for long hair. She's what? Thirty-two? Something about the brush, maybe a hollow core, amplifies each stroke so it's throaty and attention-seeking. Cheryl would have been pretty in the 1940s, that pie-face thing that for some reason rubs him wrong. Tonight she's wearing some makeup as well. Though she always applies it tastefully it has the effect of making her look slutty. Like a

librarian can look slutty. No, not the librarian—the *library*.
Like a library can look slutty.

He should slow down. He had a couple before he came
over, and this watery wine is too easy to swallow.

"Some more?" He hoists the bottle, waggles it at her back.

Cheryl meets his eye in the mirror, shakes her head and
instructively glances to her full glass on the counter beside her.

He's tired of this. All of it. Waiting, here on her couch.
Waiting as she gets dressed for work when he sleeps over;
waiting while she sautés pine nuts in her special stupid pine nut
pan as she makes them one of what he calls her adventure salads,
showing off with weird fruit in it, or quail, even goose. Waiting,
like tonight, as she pretties herself to go out. She has no TV, so
he has three choices while he waits. He can watch her leaning
at herself in the mirror. He can thumb through her coffee-table
scatter of *National Geographic*, an annual gift subscription from
her father. The latest cover is a whale in blue depths, with articles
inside on Kathmandu and "The Friendly Bacterium."

Or, strike three, he can gaze beyond her living room,
through the picture window, to a block away and the lumin-
escence of that intersection. Four Corners. There's a Four
Corners Café across the street, down the road a No Corners
Pizza—ha, ha—and a 4 Korners Kutters hair salon in the base
of her building. Surrounded by miles of farms and fields, here
two small highways happen to cross, so a collection of high-rise
condos and strip malls have gathered for no reason except this
meaningless intersection. The worst thing about it: four kitty-
corner gas stations fight for business. Gas stations should locate
for convenience, not competition, but here you have the only

four gas stations for miles glowing hard at each other, matching each other's price changes down to a fraction of a cent within minutes. Cheryl has lived at Four Corners for years, and it is maybe the worst thing about her: choosing a location whose main feature, whose only feature, is an intersection.

Cheryl claims to hate Four Corners, but at the same time it had carried a good part of their early conversations here. "I have this nice huge window," she'd said, smiling, the first time he came over, "but look what I have to look at!"

"Wow," Jack had said, shaking his head for her at those gas stations.

One time he actually saw the Four Corners' garish flare reflected on the saliva of her teeth. He saw that in some moods, the primary colours down there might scare him.

He'd added, "I bet you can see that intersection from space."

"Well, exactly. I hate it!" But chirpy, smiling. When he asked her why she'd picked this spot, she hesitated, then said, merely, "It was convenient."

She told him once that "this awful view from my wonderful window" was a contradiction that summed up her life. For three years she's been a secretary in the building where Jack works, but she claims she's saving to go to grad school, some sort of archeology. She says she's out of place at Four Corners, even suggests that it's a display of everything banal North America *lacks*. But Jack's recurring, somewhat cruel thought is that she doesn't seem out of place here at all, even though a few times she called this apartment "my aerie," as if she owned some special, eagle-eye perspective the rest of them here didn't.

"Sorry!" she says, pivoting from the mirror to roll her eyes for him. She takes a polite sip of her wine, as if to stay on the same page.

Cheryl all smiles, always.

He feels bad piling up evidence against her. He knows he's preparing for later, stoking his resolve with everything negative. He watches her, fingers teasing, elbows working. Her bathroom sounds, of tubes clicking shut and water rushing on and off, come to him now as irritation, though there had been a time, not so long ago, when such sounds were alluring, a big part of *la différence.*

He drains his wine and puts his feet up, kicking aside the yellow-framed whale. Even as he does so he feels in the gesture the chickenshit insolence that lately has been creeping into his way with her. (Hadn't Shannon done exactly that to him? Before dumping him?) Tonight he will be forthright and honest. Cheryl deserves that much.

Their first night together, Jack thought he might love her. There was that moment. They worked on different floors but had been vaguely aware of each other (they agreed) for a couple of years, and then, six months ago, against all common sense, they linked up in the bar after an office party. Later they came back here and had sex, and then he was leaving, leaning against her bedroom door frame, looking down at her. He had nothing to say and maybe he blew her a kiss. She was drowsy and snug in bundled clouds of beige comforter, her face cute in its frame of tousled hair and billowing pillows. She smiled with one side of her mouth, a smirk really, a slightly saucy look signalling a particular and private contentment. Then out of their silence, looking at him sleepy-eyed from her bed, that loveliest smirk, she whispered, "I'm the mayor of Blanketville." That's all she said, waiting for him to leave. He had never heard anyone say anything like this. I am the mayor of Blanketville. He could think of nothing good enough to say back.

"What you smiling at, Jack?"

She's watching, amused, from the bathroom. A hint of that same smirk. How do these things happen?

"Nothing."

"You're awfully patient with me. How's the wine?"

"Thin."

"That's one reason to gulp it, I suppose." Smiling, having checked out his empty glass and nearly empty bottle.

"Well, glug glug, then," he says, and pours some more.

It has to be tonight. He decided this morning after her call and her coy announcement that tonight was special and she'd made reservations at Mister Mario's. He said okay warily. Special night? They got together a half year ago. Conceivably, tonight was some sort of girly anniversary to her. Was that it? At the start they went out a month after that first time, then it was every second week for a while, and now weekends together are assumed. Cheryl is thirty-two, he is thirty-six—a dangerous age for single people, who too often settle for less. He'd warned her right off that ever since his marriage to Shannon ended, casual was all he could do until further notice. To her credit she never pushed, never spoke of a future together. But how can her future not be in her thoughts? Once you are in one of these assumed-weekend things, some notion of forever *has* to—

"Just about!" she sings from the bathroom. Something clicks shut.

"No hurry." As if for ammunition, he eyes the gas stations. She's a goddamn secretary and he's an executive, what the hell, how is that not an embarrassing cliché? Though maybe that's all he really hates here—appearances—so of course he's a shallow shit for seeing it in these terms, but what can you do?

Out the window, in a symmetry that mocks him, exactly one car sits at each of the four gas stations. Life unfolds here on rails. It is so boring. He can't help himself. "Maybe one of them will clean their windshield."

"Tonight I especially— One of who?"

It's her forcing an anniversary on him that's made him this angry, he decides. Maybe he feels some panic, that typically male thing, tonight is the sound of tires screeching to a halt, so it's all kind of funny, forgivable. Okay, how much *does* he like her? Sex is good—always for him, usually for her. Check. There's familiarity with its contempt but not too much, check. Maybe there's some love too, who knows about that? Her face is always pleasant, even sparky, check. And there's maybe a bit of something, let's call it beauty, that's more than skin-deep. She has that quirky humour he lacks—maybe that's one area where she's superior, if that's the word, check. There's her coltishness in bed that makes him shy of his own inability to make any noise. He remembers, those first times, seeing her as a young dragon when she breathed in that rough way through her widened nostrils just before she came. Check. Despite her neat-as-a-pin secretary look, and her apartment here in geometric hell, she does have a bohemian spirit, and maybe a worldliness that came from her travels with her father, who is a professor of something. Her place has primitive oddities, carved or kilned, scattered on windowsills. Some look truly fierce—scrunched faces that survived fire, lips sticking out to make a fart noise, to maybe lure another crazy, fire-hardened lover. He enjoyed that one evening going through her photo albums, and probably should have told her so. The young Cheryl on a camel. Older, launching an outrigger canoe. In one glorious shot she was maybe seventeen, brow-knit but tanned and bare-breasted, wearing a grass skirt, surrounded by scowling black kids with bellies that—

"Here we go!" she sings, and water rushes on.

The fact is, he's never been sure about her. He is nervous now. His desires knock and lurch, fighting each other.

"Ready!" she sings again, and water shuts off.

Out the window it looked windy and cold, so they walk coatless through the underground parking, at the distant end of which is a back entrance to Mister Mario's. He finds it incongruous that Four Corners not only has a high-end restaurant but that it can be accessed without going outside, and through Cheryl's garage. Jesus, he can hear a realtor assuring her, *All you need is right here in Four Corners.* But the "Mario's Lasagna" is just maybe his favourite meal of all time, plus the waiters know him now and come unasked to douse his with the spiced-oil bottle, smiling patiently because the oil is really for the gourmet pizzas.

The underground garage smells like they all do, and the cars are pathetically of a sort; her little Ford fits right in, but that's not the point. Cheryl has him gently by the right biceps, the way she likes to walk when they go out. Early on she joked how she enjoys "playing executive-girlfriend."

"So I have this surprise for you tonight." Her eyes are brown, and they go in and in.

"I've gathered."

"I was afraid you might not come if I told you what. You're such a bachelor." She tosses her hair and smiles at him, vixen of surprises.

Jesus, he was right. He should announce himself now, here in underground parking, do away with dinner altogether, but she holds open Mister Mario's door and waits for him, seeing his hesitation.

"Cheryl? Maybe—"

"Let's just go!" Mischief in her eyes, her smile is eager. "He could be here already."

"He?"

"My dad." She scowls at him. "Darling?" she mocks, cutesy, from the forties. "Tonight I'm taking you to meet my parent."

JACK'S LASAGNA IS ON ITS WAY, as is her seafood cannelloni. They've ordered already because her dad is "chronically unpredictable." She announced this proudly, like he was an artist of some sort.

"He'll be here soon."

"Why didn't we pick him up?" They're barely thirty miles from the airport.

"He actually doesn't like that. Then he'd have to worry about actually *being* there."

"Which would ruin his chronic unpredictability."

"Well, yeah. He'll take a cab." Cheryl looks away fondly. "He came home once in a helicopter. Mom was alive. We were in Montreal, the outskirts. Big loud helicopter landed in the field across the road. Highly illegal, I think."

Cheryl explains what it is her father does. Jack knows most of it. Engineer, consultant for Third World projects, helping natives do the most with the least, etc. He won a UN award. He should by rights be filthy rich but isn't. Some projects he seeded with his own money. Countries Jack had hardly heard of. Always travelling. Tonight he has a five-hour stopover and phoned Cheryl to see if they could visit.

Clearly, her father is her hero. Jack will wait and see.

They eat their salads, and Cheryl mentions a few of the trips she's taken with him. Borneo, Ivory Coast, Costa Rica several times. Jack drinks a slightly more robust pinot.

"I was really *surprised* at first," Cheryl says, remembering, chewing, "how unbelievably polluted these places are. Wherever there's lots of poor people. Dad says it's that they aren't as good as us at hiding shit." At which point she adds, as a warning, "Don't be too put off with my dad, Jack. He's not good at small talk."

"I can do more than small talk."

"No, I know, but he's … he can be direct."

"That's fine," Jack says, ruffled by the implication that he can't. Which, given his evening's plan, is maybe sort of true.

She raises her eyebrows and looks toward the door. She's been watching the door all along. She doesn't see her father much.

"You're drinking more than usual," she offers, hearing him pour.

"So?"

He plays quiet drums with two breadsticks. Cheryl says nothing, watching the door. His insolence sounded childish, but how else to respond to a comment like that? So what if he gets a bit drunk? Whenever Shannon's mother came to lurk at their place, Shannon turned prude too, went as cruel as her mother did at the faintest whiff of—

Cheryl's father is standing over him, offering his hand.

"Jack?" Cheryl stands, bubbling. She suddenly looks sixteen. "This is Simon Hodgins. Dad, this is my friend Jack Davies."

Cheryl's father nods blankly as they shake hands. He's shorter than Jack imagined, has thinning rusty hair tied back in a ponytail, and his lined face is weathered red. A rounder face even than Cheryl's, a true pie. Simon sits and turns to wave broadly at the waiter, grunting in comic desperation as he does, mumbling that he's been in fucking India for Chrissake, and needs a drink.

"Jack always gets the lasagna," Cheryl says when the waiter comes. "He says it's fantastic."

"Do you have a vegetarian version?" Simon asks the waiter.

"*You've* gone veggie?" Cheryl laughs and turns to Jack, though she keeps looking at her father. "This is a man who eats moose brains."

"*Goat* brains, please." He looks up to explain loudly to the waiter, "It was moose *nose*." Turning to Jack, he announces, one hand placed gently on his chest as if in contrition, "I have eaten a moose's *nose*. Which means I've eaten beef-flavoured sponge." He looks back up at the waiter. "Do you? Maybe a meatless lasagna? A *moose*less lasagna?"

The waiter says the chef can probably make one up and Simon smiles his thanks, nodding quickly. Jack orders a bottle of Chianti, wanting a wine that's thick and savoury. So Cheryl's father is a loud old hippie.

"No, I'm not veggie—not yet," Simon continues, as if to a general audience. "Just weaning myself off India. If I had roast beef or something tonight my gall bladder would probably blow through my rib cage. Which might get all over, ah—"

"Jack."

"—Jack."

"What were you doing in India, Dad?"

Jack eyes Cheryl, who's grinning, proud as punch of her colourful dad. Okay, well, of course. Dad is charming and funny, like award-winning humanitarians can afford to be. And as per all fathers, he thinks his daughter is perfect and deserves the best and therefore doesn't like the suitor named Ah-Jack.

Simon explains that he has been barging down a section of the middle Ganges with a frightened doctor and boxes of vaccines, checking water quality and exploring possible sites for a new kind of extremely inexpensive ground-water pump.

Cheryl announces that, speaking of the Ganges, she has to go to the bathroom. Equally deadpan, her father adopts an English accent to warn her to mind the corpses. Jack understands where Cheryl got her humour and sees how easily she rises to it. He feels his jealousy; he's out of their league in this department. Though who needs that department? Or their league?

Apropos of Cheryl being gone, Simon says, "So you're the new one."

"Well, it's been six months."

"Oh, hmm. Cheryl said there was a brand-new—" He stops. He looks at Jack steadily, eyes bright. "So that would be you. Otherwise I am eating my foot."

Over a hollowing stomach, Jack makes himself smile. He instantly tops up Simon's wine and then his own, showing nothing but confidence on his face. A joke occurs to him, perhaps in their league, about Simon's foot-eating and his gall bladder, but he has waited too long.

"Well, I can't keep up with her," her father says, blushing at the throat. "She's quite something."

"She is."

"Living up there in her aerie, keeping an eye on Mammon for me."

So that's where she got the aerie bit. And the opinion of herself. An adoring father.

"Jack. So what do you, ah—?"

"Do?" Cheryl hadn't bothered telling her father what the new one did. If in fact he was the new one. "I sell mutual funds." He meets Simon's eye. "I sell Mammon."

"Aha!"

Jack watches Simon do a good job hiding whatever contempt he feels, and this involves a scrunching of brow and a distant look. But then Simon asks, "Is it too late to buy in now, do you think?"

"Mutual funds?"

"Yes."

"Not at all."

"It's hard to know what to believe."

"Belief has nothing to do with it."

"Perhaps, yes, but let's just say, for the sake of argument, that the world economy is heading to hell in a bucket. *Again*. Mutual funds?"

"It's not."

"Well, let's just say it is." Simon dons a theatrically perplexed face, spreading his hands out to span the table. "Mutual funds, or gold?" Now he relaxes into the professorial, even raises a single finger. "Gold seems to be the thing, no? If history's any proof?"

"History doesn't count anymore. Everything's new." He can be crazy and poetic too. "Gold is an old Volvo. Funds are a Formula One race—"

"I *own* a Volvo!"

Jack briefly lifts his eyebrows as if to say, Of course you do.

"Dad! The *jimmy*!" Back from the bathroom, Cheryl stands over them, excited about something. She looks and acts younger still.

"The *jimmy*!" Simon echoes her. "Oh God, yes!"

"I'll go get it!"

"Yes! Go!"

Cheryl turns and almost runs out of Mister Mario's, out the door through which they'd come, not even looking back at Jack, like he isn't worth the time to explain.

Simon beams at something remembered, shaking his head, then notices Jack. "Has she told you about … ?"

"'The jimmy'? Um, nope."

"Jack." Simon shakes his head some more, chuckling soundlessly, watching where his daughter had gone. "Cheryl has this, this little 'artefact' I brought back from Indonesia years ago. Little island pronounced 'toot.' Practical-joke kind of gift. You've seen how Cheryl and I, um ... She hasn't shown you the jimmy?"

"Maybe. I don't think so."

"You'd know. Anyway, it's something we've come to feel bad about—about her *having*—and so, and so, since I'm going back next month, back to *Toot*, we thought I should take it back and *give* it back. I've organized a burial ceremony, actually."

Jack sits nodding. He listens to Cheryl's father go on about a people's cherished remains being looted and defiled through the centuries—Jack wants to shout, *You looted Toot?*—and how it is a crime only now being rectified.

"Even Egypt. Where did we get off robbing graveyards? No matter how grand. It's like the *more* a people revere their dead, the more we get all *horny* to find it and take it and ..."

Jack can think only of Cheryl and how abandoned he felt as she left, how he wanted to follow her up to her apartment, not stay down here with this effervescent man who makes him feel his own dullness, who speaks to him as though to a student.

Their main courses arrive and Simon groans in appreciation of "this absolute feast," a subtle attempt to remind Jack how guilty he should feel about his country's wealth and privilege. Jack says, wryly, "Hey, all you want is here in Four Corners," but Simon misses the joke, if that's what it is, and Jack knows he may have slurred a bit. Both men hover over their steaming plates waiting for Cheryl. Jack butters a bread slice, figuring to soak up some of the wine that has gotten the better of him. He watches the back door.

"I mean, Jack, what would you do if some archeologist went to your—"

"Cheryl says she wants to be an archeologist."

"Well, yes. Ethno. And she will be. Has she decided yet?"

"About …"

"If it's Dalhousie or L.A. Please tell me it's Dalhousie."

"I think it's Dalhousie."

"Good. Anyway, so what if some archeologist in, in Wales went to your great-great-grandsomebody's grave and said, 'I'll just have a scrape of *this* guy's DNA so I can see if—'"

"Did Cheryl tell you I was Welsh?"

"'Davies.' I guessed. So I can see if …"

Jack caught how he'd asked his question so hopefully. Does Cheryl even know he's Welsh? How much has he ever told her about anything? Did she tell him about going off to either L.A. or Dalhousie? Maybe.

Jack takes sips now, putting the brakes on. He chews bread. He's on the verge of making a fool of himself. He hates that he wants this man to like him. Where he wants to be is upstairs in her apartment, flipping through some pages with her, the pictures of distant shores, which would be her ethno-books of course; their shoulders are pressing, her hair draped so deliciously over them both, he can see why women are made to hide their hair in so many of those countries of hers, then she flips it all away to expose her neck to him. Mayor of Blanketville, yes. He should have asked her more questions about herself, not let her get away with being so private. And he should have told her more about himself. And about Shannon, about how another new layer of skin grows to protect from each mean flick of the tongue. About how never really listening to Cheryl is part of that thickened skin of his. He really needs most of all to tell her that his ears, and his heart, are full of skin.

"... and anyway, I see I'm ranting and rambling. The thing is, it's a *treat* not to need a translator." Old school, Simon rises from his chair a half a foot to greet his returning daughter. "And here she is."

Holding a hand reverently before her, Cheryl approaches the table carrying something small wrapped in sky-blue cloth. With a serious air she gently places the cloth on the table, near her father's plate, then carefully seats herself. Father and daughter incline their heads and murmur something. He hears Simon say something about needing a cooler, and getting it through customs.

"If we, if we ever get serious, ever get married," Jack is suddenly saying, smiling like it's a joke, looking not at them but at the far wall and its plaster frieze of gondolas, "I could pay your, your archeology. You know. School."

He hears his drunken rhythmlessness even as he speaks, then their silence. His urge had been to mischief perhaps, maybe to invade their rude intimacy. He finds himself grinning at the father. He sees the quick look Cheryl and the father share.

"Jack's been into the wine a bit, Dad," Cheryl says, blushing beautifully, eyeing her cannelloni for the first time. "You've been into the plonk, my darling," she says flatly to Jack, not looking at him. It's the second time tonight she's called him "darling," and she is being nasty.

"Yes I *have!*" Jack sings, grinning.

"Fine, Jack," Cheryl says.

"Your stupid mammony-man. The *new* one." He doesn't quite yell. A passing waiter, a young, possibly gay dude with gleaming shaven head smiles back over his shoulder at them like he understands their table completely.

Ignoring Jack, Cheryl turns to her father and nods to the blue cloth. "Anyway."

He can be direct too. He says, sternly, "Cheryl." He waits till she looks at him before he tells her, "I was going to break up with you tonight."

She stops, waits until she sees that nothing more is coming, then whispers, *"Really?"* Her father pretends to be examining the artefact now, the jimmy, but Cheryl's smiling at him, only on the one side like that, lovely, meeting his eye, not afraid of him in the slightest, never had been. Her face is aflame in humour, even delight.

So it wasn't just him being private.

Her eyes on him, he can hardly see. He loves her now, but things are probably done.

ACKNOWLEDGMENTS

Original versions of these stories appeared in the following publications: "House Clowns" in *The Malahat Review,* "Cake's Chicken" in *Fiddlehead,* "Any Forest Seen from Orbit" in *Event,* "Petterick" in *The Malahat Review,* "Geriatric Arena Grope" in *Fiddlehead,* "To Mexico" in *Numero Cinq,* "Black Roses Bloom" in *Prism International,* "At Work in the Fields of the Bulwer-Lytton" in *Numero Cinq,* and "Four Corners" in *Event.* Thank you to the editors.

Thanks to John Gould, Jay Ruzesky, Jay Connolly, Terence Young, Bill Stenson, Dede Crane, Sam Shelstad, Dave Wilson, and to Connor for the stolen chicken. Big thanks to Nick Garrison and everyone at Hamish Hamilton, and to Carolyn Forde at Westwood.